'A talented wordsmith who puts the listener right in the picture, Sarkies spins yarns that tackle relationships, bodily functions, sex, madness, child neuroses and even dyeing your pubic hair . . . a hilarious insight into Kiwi culture.'
                                    Evening Post

'He has a gift for wild, surreal and dark comedy, but surprises with touches of romanticism, wistfulness even. The man is a genius . . .'
                                    Dominion

'Some of Sarkies' work reminds the reader of a stand-up comedy routine. The pacing and timing are perfect, the sense of performance is remarkable. But a stand-up comedy routine depends on the stand-up comic to add that element of performance, to bring the narrative alive. In his short stories, Duncan Sarkies manages to do these things on the page – the words do the performing, and they engage the reader in powerful and energetic ways, so that the reader, too, contributes to the dizzying success of the whole event.'

Bill Manhire

stray thoughts and nose bleeds

Duncan Sarkies

with photos by Matt Grace

VICTORIA UNIVERSITY PRESS

VICTORIA UNIVERSITY PRESS
Victoria University of Wellington
PO Box 600, Wellington
http://www.vup.vuw.ac.nz

© Duncan Sarkies 1999

ISBN 0 86473 382 8

First published 1999

This book is copyright. Apart from any fair dealing
for the purpose of private study, research, criticism
or review, as permitted under the Copyright Act,
no part may be reproduced by any process without
the permission of the publishers

'How Bizarre' (Alan Jansson/Paul Fuemana)
Published by Universal Music Publishing Pty Ltd
Lyrics reproduced by kind permission of Universal
Music Publishing Pty Ltd

Lyrics from 'Jamaica Farewell' by Irving Burgie
are reproduced with permission

Published with the assistance of a grant from

Printed by PrintLink, Wellington

contents

wild man eyes	7
stray thoughts and nose bleeds	11
shampoo girl	16
the dandelion method	19
sad	26
the magician	32
stranger soliloquy	33
oe	38
the good thing	49
cows	56
life skills	58
18 acts of love and compassion	62
safe	106

wild man eyes

He has Wild Man Eyes. Always on the move. Always on the lookout. Eyes that cause traffic jams. Eyes that make grown men scream.

Wild Man Eyes opens his newspaper. He gazes first at the sports page, then the front page, the movies and the TV page. Wild Man Eyes pours his cornflakes into the bowl. He pours the milk into the cornflakes, and garnishes his breakfast with sliced banana and raisins.

He has Wild Man Eyes. Eyes that generate electricity. Eyes that want to eat things. Eyes that break bricks. Eyes that slice cheese.

Wild Man Eyes shakes off his pyjamas. He climbs into the shower and adjusts the controls so the water comes out not too cold, not too hot, because Wild Man Eyes likes the temperature to be just right. And as he shampoos his hair, he rubs his hands through the lather and imagines he is somewhere far far away in a distant galaxy, fighting off bad guys with quick thinking and Kung Fu.

He has Wild Man Eyes. Eyes that build dams. Eyes that lift buses. Eyes that kill sheep. Eyes that carry rocks.

Wild Man Eyes heads off to work. Another humdrum day at his humdrum job. Every minute humdrum in a sea of humdrum minutes. He looks at the photo on his desk, the studio photo of himself and his wife in nice clothes and soft focus. And as is the pattern, as is always the pattern, Wild Man Eyes dreams a different photo – a photo of Wild Man Eyes in a different land in a different world with a different job, a different wife and a different life.

   In the photo he stands proud on a bright green planet, alien love goddesses fawning at his feet, but then his boss comes in and he thinks Don't leave Don't live Sit tight Say the right things Be good and good things will come to you Don't put up with shit but be realistic Stick to what you know Meet a smile with a smile Meet a frown with a yes sir Eat well Get a haircut Don't worry Be happy Vote National Smoke outside Look busy Be right-handed Enjoy office camaraderie Take pride in the company Enjoy a challenge Praise your boss's work Praise your boss's suit Praise your boss's children Don't waste paper clips Don't waste a sick day being sick Drink beer Drink wine Don't drink wine cooler Drink when you're told Don't go home until you're told Don't drink and drive Don't squeeze the pimple Don't scratch yourself *there* No mess No fuss Stay positive Do your best Dress smart Dress bland Wear a bright tie Smell the flowers but don't talk to them Clean your desk Don't steal pens Don't read women's magazines Sign here Sign there Sign there and there and there

Remember keys Remember swipe card Remember boss's birthday Keys in right pocket Wallet in left Wash your coffee cup Wash the car Wash the dog Wash your dick Two sugars Pay your taxes Don't use the F word Remember deodorant War is bad and love is good Firm handshake Smile at children Don't do drugs Don't read cartoons Use trim milk Avoid gender-specific pronouns The best way to cure hiccups is a shock The best way to cure a headache is a fuck Don't get cancer Look interested Five-minute morning tea Half-hour lunch break Hard-fought hard-won union-negotiated fifteen-minute afternoon tea No personal calls No personal emails No personal problems during working hours Don't touch your face Don't touch her face If you want to touch your dick it's not against the law, but be discreet because the boss is in the cubicle next door Sit straight Walk tall Do right Feel small Chew your food Feed the meter Pay your share of the office Lotto ticket Pay your share of the office betting syndicate Don't demean women if there's women in the room Don't mention museums No fuss Suppress lust Suppress farts Don't jam the fax Be a good sport Know when to laugh Don't mention oil paintings Enjoy office banter Nicknames are good Use your personality to improve office morale Laugh like you mean it Brush your teeth like you mean it Comb your hair like you mean it Don't scuff your feet Stick to your wife Stick to your life Stick to what you know Routine means Stability means Steady Income means Happy Families means Life Insurance Policies means Socially Responsible means Doing Right means Good Human Being means Proud Parents means Well Liked means Love means Happiness means Comfortable means Average Non-offensive Totally Co-operative Well-meaning Well-grounded Everyday John Doe Joe Bloggs Peter Smith Andrew Brown Once loved Once lost That's life Get tough Get real No to the trip to France Yes to the retirement fund We're proud of you Well-attended funeral A good bloke One of the boys A good father A worthwhile life A happy wife Well done Did well Well to do Did right Done good Done well Well and good Thanks for the memories Here's your bonus.

He has Wild Man Eyes. Eyes that ride horses.
Eyes that scale mountains. Eyes that roam continents.
Eyes that want to be free . . .

stray thoughts and nose bleeds

You want to say, 'You are fat', but you resist the urge. Not that John is fat. You just want to say it. John is speaking about his sister's win at the raffle and there is an overwhelming desire to say, 'You're fat, John, you're fuckin grotesque', just to see what the reaction is.

You choose not to say anything, but there is a gap in conversation, which means it is your turn to speak, and you have no idea what the last sentence he said was. So you offer an 'Aaah yeah', and John says, 'Really? When was that?'

You're not sure if he's on to you or not, but you continue with the bluff: you say, 'Aaah last year', and there is another gap in the conversation because John is waiting for you to tell him about it. It is probably to do with a raffle, fairs, candy floss, schools or something related to charity in some way.

'. . . I need a new car,' you say, changing the subject, and John tells you all about auctions, and you desperately want to say, 'Fuck me, John, fuck me', not because you want John to fuck you, but because you want to know what his reaction will be. John says a sentence that finishes with 'I could introduce one to you if you like', and you want to say, 'My brain is the size of a peanut', but you resist the urge and instead say, 'That would be great.' John writes down a phone number and you put it in your pocket even though you have no idea what it is for. And now John has seen some friends.

John knows a lot of people. He introduces you to David, Michelle and Sarah, and you want to take off all your clothes to see what their reaction is but instead you shake hands and they offer you advice on how to buy a car and you say, 'When I want your advice I'll ask for it.'

Oops. You said it. You were supposed to just think it but you forgot to think and said it, and now they are looking at you like you are strange.

'Just joking,' you say, and follow that up with, 'Sorry, you have to get to know my sense of humour', and John tells them that you are going through a 'difficult patch' and that 'you are not quite yourself at the moment'.

The friends leave and say, 'Nice to meet you', and you want to say, 'I'm a creep, I'm a weirdo', but you just nod sheepishly and put your head in your hands and say, 'Sorry John', and John says, 'That's okay man', and you head to the video parlour together.

At the video parlour you desperately want to pull out a fake gun and yell, 'This is a raid, this is a fuckin raid', but instead you ask for five bucks' worth of fifties and then attempt to conquer the San Marino Grand Prix, but the steering wheel is fucked, it's gotta be the steering wheel because you are usually good at this game. There is a little kid watching as you play and you want to say, 'Fuck off, you little turd', but you drive off a bridge instead and the kid sniggers and you really want to pick your nose – nothing would give you more pleasure than picking your nose – and you could get a sneaky pick in if the kid wasn't watching, so you say, 'Fuck off, kid, I want to pick my nose', and that was a bad idea because his big brother who is a member of White Power is moving toward you and it's time to go now so you say, 'John, let's go, let's fuckin go', and you both go.

John says, 'What is it with you, man?' and you want to say, 'Help me, John, help me', but you say, 'I think I should be alone', so he lets you go and says, 'I'll call you', and you say, 'That'd be nice.'

And you walk on the beach and look at the waves crashing in as loads of proud mums and dads play with their kids and you want to scream, 'Somebody give me a hug!' but instead you sit on a vacant patch of beach which is calming and relaxing until a kid disturbs your peace by throwing sand in your face because kids like to do stuff like that.

You do not say, *'I'm going to break your bones, you little fuckwit.'*

You just sit there and rub the sand from your eyes, give him the evil eye, but he pokes his tongue out and you're about to do something stupid, so it might be time to go again . . .

So you go home and because there is no one else home you can at last pick your nose, and it feels good, but you never know when to stop, do you, and now it is bleeding, so you go to the bathroom and the blood drips into the sink and you shove toilet paper up your nostril and think about getting a job at the circus.

Because you are at home alone you yell in an American Mafia accent, 'You bustin my balls? You bustin my balls?' which has no context and makes no sense but 'Who cares?' you say as you undo your belt buckle, drop your trousers and yell, 'I am a sea lion, and sea lions don't wear trousers!' in a thick Scottish accent.

You go to the lounge and read the newspaper but your nose blood drips on to the couch, leaving a big fat stain, and advertising states that Cold Water Surf removes blood, but the couch will not fit into the washing machine.

You announce out loud in a plum English accent, 'I have left my mark on the world!' and then in an Indian accent, 'Hygiene has a lot to answer for', as you clean up by pouring salt all over it, which doesn't work – so much for old wives' tales . . . The toilet paper in your nostril feels full, so you pull it out and put it in the ashtray next to the old fag-ends, fingernails, used bandages and other grimy build-up that you must get around to cleaning up some day. You stuff some new bog paper up your nose and look at the bathroom mirror, and in your best German accent you announce, 'The truly grotesque are as beautiful as the truly beautiful!' You go to the pantry and open a tin of raspberry jam, you mix it with milk until it is glupy and disgusting, and you smear it all over your face. Then you start crying.

You could dial 111 and yell down the line, '*Help me, self-inflicted nose bleed!*' but instead you phone John and say, 'John, I think you'd better come over', and he says he'll be round in a tick.

And John is as good as his word, because here he is a tick later, bringing you a glass of water, and you say to him, 'I'm not coping, man, I'm not coping', and he wets a cloth and cleans you up and says, 'It's okay, man, I'm here', and he rocks you gently back and forth and you want to say, 'Thank you Mummy', but instead you say, 'Don't say that, don't say that', and then you say, 'Thank you Mummy', and then you say, 'I told you not to say that', and John just laughs because he's seen it all before. He keeps on rocking you back and forth and repeats, 'It's okay, it's okay, it's okay', and you screw your face up as tight as it can go and a mixture of tears and blood drip off the tip of your nose onto your jersey.

In a few hours' time you are calm again. John hands you a cup of tea and you say, 'Thank you', and he says, 'Any time', and you want to say, 'You're the best friend I ever had', but sentiment has never been your strong suit, so you say, 'Did you watch the footy?' instead.

And the two of you drink cups of tea and analyse the merits of the country's top centre three-quarters and then you yarn about the World Cup, and then you yarn about the America's Cup, and then the Davis Cup, and it's all squashed up in a little marble in the back of your head now, all squashed up, all hidden away, out of harm's way for another day. And you smile and John sighs, because you both know you'll do it all again tomorrow.

shampoo girl

Think of shampoo commercials and the woman in the shower with bouncy hair. The woman with bouncy hair is happy. It springs back and forth. She is strong. She is attractive. See how it sways in the breeze. See how it flicks from side to side. See how she glows in her business clothes. She is happy that her teeth are bright and shiny. She is American. She is the dream girl. She is kind and caring. Slow motion silky smooth. She moans in the shower. She is happiest there. Smells like aloe vera. She is beautiful in her towel. Wears lipstick and looks good by the lake. Stands under the waterfall like an angel.

    Today her scalp feels sore, like someone's playing tug-of-war with every strand and every pore. Skin slowly stretched like cellophane too tight. No colour in her cheeks, just an off-putting off-white. All the product in the world cannot cure this, girl.

She goes to the doctor and he feels her head and next she is whisked into a large white room where a man in green shaves her head, and off it all comes, drops to the floor, itches her back, screams 'No more, no more.'

And now she is bald and it is there for all to see. A pimple on her head. A pimple never seen before. The pimple says, 'It's nice up here, I'll pitch my tent, I'll pay no rates, I'll pay no rent, I make the rules and the rules are simple, I'm here to stay, I'm the penance pimple and I'll make you pay.' And the third doctor frowns and the fourth doctor sighs and the fifth doctor agrees with the ninth doctor's point of view that 'It is sad, very sad, there's not a lot that we can do.' So she smiles and says, 'Thank you' and the tenth doctor says, 'Chemotherapy is the only cure', but she does not answer because she has walked out the door.

And she sits at home and stares into the mirror and watches another pimple growing, and another, and another – rise and shine, it's pimple time. The new letter says she should see a 'specialist' and it brings her to tears and she scowls, 'Not now, not tomorrow, not in a million years . . .'

So she goes to the place of her finest hour, off with her clothes and into the shower, and applies enriching enhancing energising empowering anti-dandruff shampoo, but it makes her sick: she is sick in the shower, she is sick in the loo, sick on her leg, sick on her towel, sick on her body ointment, skin treatment, conditioner, moisturiser, mousse, make-up and facial accessories . . .

And as she rubs her scalp she lets out a scream; her eyes have turned black, her skin off-cream, her blood bright red as she curses the god with the sick sense of humour who has carved out a tumour all over her head.

And she lies on the floor and waits to be dead.

There she lies on the floor and the shower is still going and the plug's in the bath and the bath's overflowing, but she doesn't care, she could lie another year. 'It does not matter,' she sings to herself. 'Here I will wait for as long as it takes. Here I will lie till the day that I die', and she lies there singing while the phone is ringing, and her answerphone voice sounds shrill and naïve as her agent excites with 'They want *you* to be the *new* face of fabric softener in Pakistan, India, Sri Lanka, Indonesia', and she laughs and thinks, 'When it rains it pours and when it pours it stinks.'

And she stares at her face on the shampoo bottle, and her face gives a smile, saying, 'How do you do?' She looks it in the eye and pleads, 'I am you, I am you', but her reflection looks back, says, 'That ain't true.'

She has written in her will that the shampoo bottle shall not get chucked in the bin; it will go to her next of kin and be forever preserved, to sit in their bathroom and be forever observed.

Now the bottle sits there on the bathroom shelf of her sister's husband's nephew's ex-partner's house, and no one looks at her, no one notices she is there, but there she is – the unbiodegradable plastic keeps her looking fantastic. If you go to the loo she's in your peripheral view, smiling down at you; and if you read very carefully you can learn that the ingredients are water, sodium, laureth sulfate, cocanidophopyl, betaine, dimethanol, sodium glutenate, glycol distearate, panthonol, fragrance, potassium sorbate, guar hydroxypropyl trimonium chloride, sodium citrate, tocophenyl acetate, CI 19140, CI 16255; and above all of that she is there with her smile and her long flowing hair.

See how it bounces in the breeze. See how it flicks from side to side. Teeth bright and shiny. She is American. She is the dream girl. Kind and caring. Slow-motion silky smooth. Smells like aloe vera. Beautiful in her towel. Looks good by the lake. Stands under the waterfall like an angel.

the dandelion method

1. Pretend to like the smell of flowers. Pretend to appreciate them in all forms. Appreciate the colours. Appreciate the soft petals and the prickly stems. Love every part of the flower. Love all flowers. Even daisies and dandelions. If there are people around, sit near a bunch of dying flowers, and look at them in such a way that it looks like you are *appreciating* them.

2. Enjoy the ocean. Enjoy waves crashing in. Enjoy the forces of nature and the ebb and flow and the sheer power of it all. All coastlines are interesting. If you like only fine golden sandy beaches you will appear *fickle*. If you appreciate rugged weather-torn coastlines you will come across as someone who appreciates the *cyclic* nature of life. Find some rugged coastline, and sit on the ugliest rock. Some strangers will see you ahead of them. They

will assume you are having deep thoughts. This is good. For the most interesting thoughts, choose craggy rocks.

3. Change your hairstyle. Dye it a subtle red, and pretend to be a natural redhead. (Dye your pubes too.)

4. Walk around town like a 'lost soul, searching for answers'. Do this for two weeks.

5. Ask the girl who works at the petrol station out on a date. Take her to the rock. Tell her you used to be gay, but seeing her has 'reopened your heterosexual door'. Look into her eyes as she looks at the sea. Get her to open up about her childhood. When she has done this, you can kiss her. Don't get too busy with your hands, and hold off on the tongue – you must appear to be tender and thoughtful enough to have the larger issues on your mind. Seedy hotel rooms were made for sex. Large rocks are for kissing. Don't get these mixed up, or you will need to see a psychiatrist.

6. Have sex with the petrol attendant after work in one of the cars in the garage. (If there is a Mercedes around, use that.) Make it look like the idea to do this came to you on a whim. You will appear *spontaneous* and a little *wild*.

7. After two months, break up with the petrol pump girl. (Say you can't get your old boyfriend out of your head.)

8. Become close 'friends' with another woman (vocation optional), and tell her you are having a hard time getting over a previous relationship.

9. Sit on the rock with your new friend. The rock will feel *different* now. Sit reflectively. Analyse out loud where the relationship went wrong. Assess out loud your own failings in the relationship.

Your friend will be impressed by your ability to share *weakness*, which is a strength. If you feel she is suitably impressed, give her a kiss, but make it feel like she kissed you. This is not easy, but if you put your face in close proximity to hers and leave it there for a minute or two, eventually she will take the lead. This way your chances of a successful 'no consequences' fling are much higher. It will also give the impression that you are *vulnerable*.

10. Buy sunglasses. Buy a newspaper. Read the newspaper in a public place, near to where your new friend works. Allow her to spot you, then tell her you are 'too emotional to talk right now' and would rather be 'left alone to read the news'. Make a date to meet her in twelve days' time.

11. Take your new friend to the Gardens. Appreciate the flowers together. Break down in front of some dandelions. (Remember to refer to them as 'the beautiful weed'.) Your friend will hug you beside the dandelions. This will feel nice. Apologise for your outburst of emotion and explain that the flowers remind you of your childhood. If she asks for specifics, just say you are 'too close to it to talk'. You will appear *complex* and *fascinating*.

12. Have sex with your friend in her car. Make it look like you are releasing ten years of pent-up energy. Make sure the car is not parked near a school. For an especially romantic experience, try doing it on the outskirts of a remote farm. If there are cows nearby, acknowledge them after you have had sex. Your friend will be impressed that after such a *spiritual* moment you are still able to care about the welfare of animals.

13. As you drive home, talk about Amnesty International and shed a tear for the political dissidents of a South American country.

14. If you can cook, cook your friend a meal. If you can't cook, go to the supermarket and buy impressive exotic ingredients, but in a fit of passion rip off your clothes and make love just before you were meant to start cooking. Then lie in bed and say you're not hungry any more.

15. It is time to break up, as your friend will soon realise how shallow you are. To do this, leave town, saying you 'need time alone in the wilderness'.

16. Go to a medium size tourist town (ideal population 9000). Meet a backpacker from Canada. Remark on the mountainous landscape of Canada. Your new friend will talk about the landscape of New Zealand. Reply that 'it has nothing next to the landscape of Canada'. Have a mock heated argument on whose country is better. (Because you are sticking up for a different country, this will make you appear *giving*.)

17. Have a spa together. Get into the spa naked, and explain 'that's what everyone does here in New Zealand'. With any luck, she will do the same. Do not gulp or ogle. Pretend this is an everyday situation. If you are having trouble pretending this, imagine that she has clothes on and the two of you are sitting in a cafe. Have patience. Do not touch the backpacker. Do not let the conversation drift to a sexual nature. Do not hide your genitals unless aroused, in which case hide your genitals whilst trying to make it look like you are not hiding your genitals.

18. Discuss world politics (for good results choose the situation in Tibet). Find out the backpacker's favourite movie. Find out the backpacker's favourite flower. (Remember – your favourite is 'the beautiful weed'.) Find out the secret place the backpacker goes when she needs to be alone. Reply with, 'That's amazing. Me too.'

the dandelion method   23

19. Get dressed, while continuing normal conversation. The sheer normality of this will make the backpacker assume this is common New Zealand practice, and that you are not attracted to her, which will attract her to you.

20. Hire a car, and with your new backpacker friend, drive to a climbable mountain. (Select very carefully.) Climb halfway up the mountain, and then say to the backpacker, 'This reminds me of the first time I made love.' (Remember – this should be the first time you have talked about sex in any way.) When the backpacker inquires, say it merely reminds you in the *metaphysical* sense. Then stare at the backpacker for another ten seconds, apologise, and walk to the top of the mountain. At the top of the mountain, discuss 'the rat race', 'perspective', and let slip that you enjoy feeding ducks. Admit that you realised halfway up the mountain that you have *feelings* for her.

21. Get to the bottom of the mountain without falling off. Choose a steeper descent, and use the difficult bits as an opportunity to hold hands. Let her help you more than you help her – this will make you appear *feminist*. When you get to the bottom, have a twenty-minute breather, before the next step.

22. Make love to the backpacker in your rental car at the bottom of the mountain. Remember the handbrake.

23. Spend quality time in motel rooms with the backpacker. Laugh at how funny it is that she has come to the 'land of scenery' and is spending all her time inside motel rooms. Because the relationship is clearly not going to last, you should make love at least three or four times a day, if you have the energy.

24. Wait for her to split up with you. When she does, appear sad, and talk longingly of 'visiting her in Canada'. See her off at the

airport. If you are good at crying on demand, do so – it will make you appear *sensitive* to other people in the airport lounge.

25. Write an apology letter to one of your first ever girlfriends. Explain in the letter that you have just walked past some dandelions and have been thinking about her 'ever since'. Tell her you are *mature* now. Insist on visiting her – word it in such a way that she will assume it to be a 'platonic friendship thing'.

26. Go to the SPCA, and pick up a puppy. Spend two weeks befriending the puppy. Name the puppy 'Chris'.

27. Visit your ex-girlfriend in her home town. Go to her home. Let her fall in love with your puppy. Discuss openly your new-found maturity. Shake hands with her husband and say, 'I've been looking forward to meeting you.' Play with her kids for as long as it takes. Listen attentively to anything they say, no matter how boring. Just before tea time, show them some magic tricks and get them to perform a special 'magic show' for their parents.

28. At the dinner table, do not eat your steak. Explain that you are a vegetarian now, but that you also believe in freedom of choice, so you are relaxed about them 'eating meat' around you. From your bag, unwrap a chickpea burger (you can buy these at some supermarkets, but pretend you cooked it yourself), and feed it to the puppy. Let the kids fall in love with the puppy.

29. When you are finally alone with your ex-girlfriend, break down and say, 'The time I was with you was the best in my life.' Admit that you are unhappy. Say you are happy that she is happy. When she says she is not happy, whisper to her, 'Meet me in my car at 11:10.'

30. Make love to your ex-girlfriend in your car, but withdraw before orgasm and say, 'I'm sorry, this just isn't right.' When she says, 'Why?' talk about what a fine man her husband must be, and say you don't want to 'mess things up'. Then stare into her eyes for ten seconds. Appear to be holding back from crying. Then say, 'I love you. I've always loved you', and kiss her passionately. Then do what comes naturally, but be careful of the car horn.

31. Leave early the next morning. Remember to take Chris (your dog) with you. Say to your ex-girlfriend, 'It's for the best.' She will nod in agreement.

32. Drive to a big city. Get a flat. Get a normal haircut. Get a commerce-related job.

33. When Chris gets too much of a handful, release him in a park with lots of children, put up some obligatory 'lost dog' notices, but put the wrong phone number on the notices. Appear sad in all the places you used to walk the dog. Accept consolation food parcels from concerned old ladies.

34. Work hard for ten months, and live like a monk so you can 'charge up the old batteries' and 'get the energy to love again'. If you have a video, this might be a good time to build up a collection of pornographic movies.

35. It is now time to get out of the big city. Go to a coastal town of approximately 5000 people, and return to step 1. (Remember to choose a new set of towns this time round, because at the old ones you are no longer welcome.)

sad

He is sad.

He wants the world to know he is sad, but he keeps smiling and giving public displays of mild happiness. He has tried walking about sullen – to communicate his sadness more effectively – but this seems to achieve little. When he does this he is pretty much ignored by everybody. He has contemplated doing a less subtle version of sullen – perhaps a few tears at a public gathering – but he considers this to be grandstanding; and besides, he does not have the ability to time his sadness for optimum results. So he smiles and chit chats, and when someone asks him, 'How are you?' he answers, 'Fine', which he is not.

He curses the world for not noticing his sadness. If they were more alert – if we were all more alert – we could spot each other's sadness; we could do something about it – offer a helping hand, an occasional 'You're great' or, for the really keen, an in-depth counselling session.

Counselling. An ugly word. A New York word. Counselling is an everyday thing in a Woody Allen movie, but in New Zealand counselling has *stigma*. He wants a friend to counsel – or is it console? – him, but not in a way that feels like counselling. He would like the friend to outpour some of their grief too, so they can remain on similar vulnerability levels.

Death is useful for sadness. When death happens you can be publicly sad – people will come to your aid after a death. But what do you do when there is no death? No scandal? No obvious mitigating circumstance? He is just sad. Very, very sad.

He phones his friend – his special friend – the one he does not mind communicating if not sadness then at least the occasional whine to; he hopes his friend can handle the transition from the occasional whine to genuine sadness. This is a risk, because if she – his friend is a she – can't, then the friendship will be stained by his outpouring of sadness. His friend may no longer look upon him as 'someone to have a good time with'; his friend may stop inviting him to go to such-and-such's place, to have nice walks on overcast days; worst of all, his friend might stop phoning him *as often* as he phones her, creating an imbalance that his ego will have a hard time dealing with.

He phones his friend and gets the answerphone. It is an amusing answerphone message, but this does not cure his sadness (although points for trying). He takes it as a sign that he shouldn't communicate his sadness to this friend, so he goes back to his room and lies in bed, looks at his white walls – white is the boringest colour for walls – and cries. At least, he attempts to cry. In the same way someone attempts to throw up by sticking half their hand down their throat, he is attempting to induce crying by thinking *especially hard* how *bad* everything is, how *really really bad* things are, but he fails because crying is not something he is good at, so the tension stays within him, crushing, tightening from the inside . . .

Oh for a massage, a nice massage – not too hard, not too soft, tender but not too tender – from preferably a woman. He knows there is nothing gay about having a massage from a male friend, but he couldn't possibly do it without imagining all his old school friends there in a line, watching, sniggering as he receives a massage from a *bloke*. No, it must be a woman – a beautiful woman ideally, so he can fool himself that the massage is not a form of counselling, but a form of *sensuality* – but any woman will do, so long as she falls into the acceptable 'five years either side of his age' range. He needs to call his friend and ask her for a massage, but it's bound to sound *forward*, so he tells himself his age-old theory: that tension is good for the body; that people who get massages get addicted to them; they become aware whenever they haven't had one for two days so they pester those around them for *another* massage, and *another* one, and Oh, since you happen to be sitting near to me, how about *another* one, because I can feel a knot in my 'fibula' – or 'cortis biopti' – or some other infinitesimal muscle that no normal person has heard of. These people are a burden to society – if he actually phones someone and asks for a massage, he will be submitting to their *touchy feely* ways, and he has far too much integrity for that.

Maybe he should be sad outside. That would be romantic. He walks outside and sits, looks at the beautiful view – the ocean, the trees wavering in the wind, the cold wind; it is a very cold wind, not a very comfortable place to be sad. So he goes inside, gets a jacket, comes back out and finds a more sheltered spot, but all the sheltered spots have lousy views – and what's the point of being sad in a hole underneath the house, staring at your flatmate's bicycle? – so he takes off his jacket and goes inside, lies on his bed, and looks at the time.

It is 5:43. This is bad news. This means he has been sad for only half an hour. There is much more time in the day to fill with sadness. He could fill it by sleeping, but he is too sad to sleep, so he tries television, but there's not anything good on – there's never anything good on – and unlike most people he is far more aware of quality programming when he is sad.

How about some delusions of suicide? They are always a good cure for sadness. So he imagines killing himself. He chooses pills because the other alternatives involve physical pain, which he is not very good at, even when imagining. He focuses more on everyone's reaction to his suicide – which is of course extreme – and this brings a smile to his face. Then he ends the daydream by telling himself that suicide would be the easy way out and gives himself a pat on the back for not being a coward. At last, his energy now restored, he has a burst of crying: a good cry – one of those nice quiet ones where you're pretending you're trying not to cry but your sadness is so intense that you *can't help it*. He feels like Vincent Van Gogh about to chop his ear off. Sadness and art go hand in hand.

So he picks up his guitar, waiting for a burst of heartfelt blues, but sadness can't disguise ability – and all he can muster is a D, C, G7 riff with the lyrics *I feel baad, a raw pain in my haad*, which doesn't quite cut it. So he sings, *Well I'm sad to say, I'm on my way, I won't be back for many a day, My heart is down, my head is turning around, I had to leave a little girl in Kingston Town* – and he puts the guitar down, utterly disgusted with himself.

He has a shower – which has helped his sadness in the past – but this time he doesn't feel remotely better until he applies the conditioner, and even that does not have its usual effect. Out of the shower and back into the same clothes, he ponders his options – Go Outside and Face the World – Use the Phone – Do a Poo – Go to Bed.

He goes to bed and stares at his fuckin white walls, and he is getting annoyed now because he is having a difficult job sustaining his sadness, and if he's struggling now what's he gonna be like when he sees the world again? He concentrates once more on the things that made him sad, but struggles to remember what they were. Then he remembers, almost cries, and in a burst of energy he puts on some new clothes and heads out to see the world, so that they can be impressed by his 'I just cried half an hour ago' look – which of course he will pretend to disguise badly with a warm smile and feigned good spirits.

Only his act is too convincing. The first person he runs into is the Indian man from the dairy – and he can't be sad to the Indian man from the dairy – so he has an interesting conversation about cricket and what is wrong with the New Zealand team, before heading on his way into town.

In town he can find no one to be sad at. Where are all his friends? He goes to all the places they usually hang out: the cafes, movie theatres, video game parlours, the supermarket – where he buys a pottle of mussels, eats three and tips them back into the rubbish bin – and the main street, where he walks up and down and up and down and up and down and where is everybody? Hellooo – I'm saaad – Hellooo – It's meeee – I'm saaad – Where is everybodeee?

He runs into a girl he used to go to university with three years ago, but by now his eyes have dried up to the point that his fellow university student says to him, 'You look great. What have you been up to lately?' And he says, 'This and that, I've been working out my income tax', and they both agree that tax is a shit, and then it's 'Nice to catch up with you' and she's off, freshly perked up by a happy chirpy happy chirpy happy conversation with an old face from the past, and she's sure to tell her friends about him – 'Oh yes, he's doing so well for himself, he looked really happy.' Blew it again.

He goes to the pub – by himself – and drinks an awful amount of beer, but by the time he finally does run into friends he is so happy to see them that he tells jokes and funny stories and they sing old eighties songs and laugh and smile, and a good time is – unfortunately – had by all.

He is at home again now. It has been a happy night. He drinks a glass of milk – he has heard it prevents throwing up – before heading to bed, where he lies, stares at the dark, and once more feels alone with his thoughts, alone with the world, neutral.

He knows it is inevitable, and feels himself being filled up again – like there is a leak in the roof and it's dripping into his brain, into his back, into his heart; his eyes well up again as he wishes he was somewhere else, someone else, with someone else. And as the window makes the noise windows do when they haven't been closed properly, and the regular sound of traffic outside disappears to just the occasional sound of some drunken hoons; as the clock ticks on from 1:55 to 1:56 to 1:57 to 1:58 – he wearily, softly, beautifully cries himself to sleep.

the magician

One could never question her commitment. She has bought 52 packets of playing cards. At $4.95 a pack, the trick has cost her a total of $257.40. She has removed all the tens of spades and put them together in a pack. She asks a friend, a random friend to pick a card, any card, and he does. Straight away she guesses, 'Is it the ten of spades?' Her friend is well and truly satisfied, but she did not do it for him, she did it for magic. She will sleep well tonight.

stranger soliloquy

A man walks down the street.
He is going to die.
We are all going to die.
He is going to die in ten minutes' time.

Don't be sad.
You don't know him.
Even if you did know him, you wouldn't be *that* sad.
You wouldn't have missed him.
You might have noticed he wasn't there.
You might have thought he was overseas.
You might have thought he'd gone to Australia.
If he'd gone to Australia you would be happy.

Australia is a nice place.
Warm climate.
You should be happy.
If he was in Australia you would be happy.

A man walks down the street.
He is going to Australia.

That's better, isn't it?
He's probably lying on a beach.
He'll get some toy koalas from the souvenir shop.
He'll go night clubbing.
He'll go to a strip show.
They like that sort of thing over there.
He's probably off to Sydney to become gay.
That's typical.
He doesn't deserve to go to Australia.
Let him die here.
The world is better off without him.
Let him die in a cold dark room.
Deserves what he gets.

A man walks down the street.
He is going to die.

That's better.
Everyone gets their just deserts.
Although it's his parents' fault.
It always is.
He was probably abused as a child.
They all are.

Probably abused with an iron.
Poor man.
Never stood a chance.
If you treat someone like an animal then they become an animal.
He needs love.
Tenderness.
A friend.
You should invite him round to dinner.

A man walks down the street.
You invite him round to dinner.
He looks at you funny.

As if he can judge.
Pot calling the kettle black.
He probably smokes pot.
They all do.
He's not welcome.
You tell him you've changed your mind.
You tell him to stop staring at you funny.

A man stands on the street.
He's staring at you funny.

You tell him to Go Fuck Himself.
He's staring at you, like you're funny.
He is making you go red.
You tell him to Fuck Off Back To Australia.
He is still staring at you, like you're funny.
You tell him you will Find Out His Address, Shit On His Doorstep, and Murder His Kids.

A man runs down the street.

He is a Cry Baby.
What a Cry Baby he is.
He is making you feel guilty.
He is making you feel *mean*.
You run after him to apologise.

A man runs down the street.

He is running very fast now.
He is a good runner.
He is hard to keep up with.
He is very good over long distances.
You know what they say about long-distance runners.
Long-distance runners are patient people.
Patient people are kind to their mothers.
People who are kind to their mothers make good husbands.
You could do with a husband.

A man runs down the street.
You shout to him, Will you marry me?
It's hard to run and propose at the same time.
He doesn't hear you, so you scream it at the top of your voice.
He doesn't appear to be able to hear you.
Perhaps he is deaf.
Perhaps he is in a rush.
He doesn't seem to be able to hear you.

A man sprints down the street.
You scream, Will you marry me!

He is stuck at some traffic lights.
He is in an awful hurry.
He crosses the street even though the lights are green.
He is not looking where he is going.
He runs across the street, and is hit by a bus.
Best you be on your way now . . .

A man lies under a bus.
He lies under the tyre of a bus.

Don't be sad.
You don't know him.
Even if you did know him, you wouldn't be *that* sad.
You wouldn't have missed him.
You might have noticed he wasn't there.
You might have thought he was overseas.
You might have thought he'd gone to Australia.

A man lies under a bus.
He has gone to Australia.
That's the way things go.

oe

He never liked it. Harmless, mindless, repetitive chorus, bubblegum pop with extra cheese. A Kiwi classic hit. Still, there it was, on the airport monitor, and there was no denying – the singer was right.

> *Pele's in the back,*
> *Sweet Zina's in the front,*
> *Cruisin down the freeway,*
> *in the hot hot sun . . .*

And after he and his mate had settled into the shitty hotel room, gone to their first coffee shop, bought a joint from the guy behind the bar, sat down, and smoked the fucker *legally*, the song comes back on the TV again.

Pele preach words of comfort,
Zina just hides her eyes,
Policeman taps his shoulders,
Is that a Chevy 69?
How bizarre, how bizarre . . .

OMC on MTV. He can't take his eyes off the screen. It's like someone is massaging his eyes and his cerebral . . . thoughts getting lost half . . . new people he's never seen walk . . . eat some crisps, salt and vin . . . play video games, soccer set in the future, planet Jupiter, and the score is . . .

And him and his mate can't believe that they are doing this in public and everyone is *visibly* wasted. Not like back home where it's all Hush Hush Pretend You're Straight Here Come the Cops Just Act Normal . . . And there's a couple of Kiwis now, outside the window – his mate recognises them, and these guys are munted, they've hired bicycles, but they can't even get on the fuckers, they are laughing and drooling like school children having the time of their lives . . .

It's like Amsterdam was designed for optimum viewing pleasure for the stoner tourist: sex museums – art museums – torture museums – architecture in every direction – he can feel the history bearing down on him like a fuckin collapsed tent – no personal space here – and check this out – the Men's is ultraviolet, ultra-fuckin-violet so that the bowl glows and the bog-roll glows and his piss is fuckin luminous, a bog so perfect he has to christen it in the purest sense, and he enjoys every second of it, every fuckin . . .

And his mate's scared, cos some Turkish guy pulled a gun on him – it wasn't a real gun, it was prob'ly two fingers pointed out his jacket pocket, but his mate's not taking any chances, man, he would've stayed out of that block for the whole fuckin holiday if the streets hadn't been so fuckin circular and he wasn't so stoned and oh no here we go, there he is again and let's go this way, and fuckin walk quickly, man, let's get outta here, and they need a piss so they go to McDonald's and it costs them a dollar and what is it with this town, man, this is fucked, it's fucked, it's just . . .

The prostitutes are beautiful, it's like walking through the aisles at Foodtown except the produce is staring at him, willing him, and tap a tap tap hellooo she's talking to you, and he's half drawn because beautiful women don't look at him *that way*, but he thinks of diseases and his girlfriend and he counts to ten and walks with his head down, and he trips on a bit of the road that's not big enough to trip on, and a guy comes past and whispers 'Coke LSD Ecstacy' in his ear and if his mate wasn't with him he'd be scared, he'd be fuckin shitting himself, and he walks and freaks and thinks, Get it together get it together get it . . .

The trip has been a blur. A big gigantic blur. Fuck knows what Amsterdam *actually* looks like – current impressions are City of Confusion, City of Disorientation, City of Fear, City of Lost Thoughts. It's time to get out of here – they leave with regrets – they didn't try space cake and they booked the ferry at the same time as the All Blacks test, and they're slutted cos they found a pub that's playing it and now there's an empty hole where the Tri Nations series was gonna be . . .

And they are running early and nothing's worse than running early so they share one last joint and then they're running late, and he trips down the stairs spilling all his fuckin oh no luggage and he'd pack it faster but he finds the situation kinda fascinating and has to pause a second to take in the wonder of it all and how rich life can be and his mate sprints ahead to get the train, leaving him struggling with his big quintessential fuckin ton-of-bricks backpack when he realises . . . he realises . . . ohhh Jesus. Jesuuuus . . .

Flashback time and he remembers leaving Auckland, mocking –

'You've been suckered in by the whole tourist thing' – his mate for getting a money belt, but in retrospect it had been handy, so handy he'd asked his mate to store his passport and his travellers' cheques and his money and his plane tickets in it . . . End of flashback and he's in the train station looking up at the thingywhatsit with all the times of the trains and fuck knows where his mate is, he's left abandoned like some kind of mutant stoned orphan, alone in Amsterdam, no money, no passport, with a huge backpack that's screaming 'steal me, steal me' to every fuckin pimp and drug dealer and child-abuser in sight, and just as another dealer whispers 'Coke Ecstacy Acid Ecstacy' in his ear he's overcome by the weight of the million-ton fucker, and he's on his back now, doing dead ants in the middle of the Amsterdam train station and life ain't pretty at this moment in time, life is not . . .

He takes some pleasure in the perfect badness of it all. If you're gonna have a bad experience might as well do it properly, and this is definitely a defining moment and we need defining moments, otherwise we can't define ourselves and that's a positive and where the fuck is he, where the fuck is he, and there he is, he's here, he's back, he's back, thank fuckin whatshisname, God, thank him and bless me bless you bless this moment cos they don't get much . . .

They're back at the regular now. His mate says, 'I would never have left you, man', and of course it's obvious when he thinks rationally, but say goodbye to that cos here's another joint, this one was grown in the West Indies, his mate saw a place that sells imported New Zealand hash – 'Now if that's not fuckin ironic then nothing is' – and they laugh like mental patients because now it's all good news, they'll get to watch the All Blacks, they'll get to travel on the night ferry, and they get to try space cake – which fills the gap – one needs to experience a true state of paralysis to appreciate the basic things in life, like walking and talking and moving your arms and the ability to *think* from time to time, and the ability to take your eyes away from the fuckin TV set and look who's playing:

> Ooh Baby (Ooh Babaaay)
> It's makin me crazy (Makin me crazaaay)
> Every time I look around
> It's in my face . . .

'How Bizarre' is number three in Europe, and there he is, their Kiwi friend, smiling from the TV set like some kind of catchy songsmith God, observing their every step, and it occurs to him that Pauly Fuemana from OMC is Aslan from *The Lion, the Witch, and the Wardrobe*, watching over them, keeping them safe, his mane glowing in the sunset, and he wants to tell his mate this but the thought dissolves when his mate says, 'Let's go to the game.'

And they're at the pub screaming at the top of their lungs as the Aussie No.8 punches Frank Bunce 1 2 3 4 5 6 7 8 times in the head and Frank Bunce just laughs, and they're screaming 'off, off, off' and the Aussies are cheering, and the Dutch are mocking them in Dutch but fuck them, it's the national game and it's the best fuckin high they've had since being here, especially when Mehrts plays a blinder second half and that was one of *the greatest* come-from-behind victories ever. Fitzy says the usual things, all credit, our boys gave a hundred and ten percent, a game of eighty minutes, and special thanks to those two supporters in Amsterdam, without you boys we never would've won and could you score us some skunk cos we . . . is he really saying that or is that . . . where are we, is this . . . the walls of the pub are red but he can't tell because the inside of his eyelids are black.

He's in Scotland now, his mate's just pissed off down to London and he's about to embark on an epic little journey, stay with a cool doctor chick in Liverpool, an old Pommy mate in Birmingham, and then check out Dublin if the money hasn't run out. And it's morning, say eleven o'clock, and he's sleeping in because sleeping in is twice as enjoyable when you're overseas, and there's a phone call for him and it's his girlfriend from the other side of the world and she says, 'I've got some news' . . .

And it's obvious it's a death so he scans through the list of dead people it might be: Mum, Dad, Uncle John, Patrick, Mr O'Hagan from across the road, *she's pregnant*. That's not as bad as a death. But it's bigger than a death. It's not what he's expecting . . .

How pregnant? Three and a half months. Jesus. It's defining moment time again and he asks the right questions like, 'Are you all right?' and 'What do you want to do?' and says 'wow' and 'Jesus' and 'wow' and 'Jesus' and 'wow' and 'Jesus' and there's some nitty-gritty – abortion (too far gone – not an option) and adoption (her gut feeling is no, he won't tell her his) – he gets off the phone and announces 'Guess what, I'm gonna have a baby', and laughs at the ensuing silence around him, and what's that noise? It sounds innocuous, coming from the back room, someone's stereo switched on, and *da na na, da na na, da na na, na naaa* . . .

Elephants and acrobats,
Lion snakes monkey,
Pele speaks righteous,
Sister Zina says funky
How bizarre, how bizarre . . .

The song is a work of genius. The chorus rebounds inside the walls of his head like a fly trying to get out a window. He thinks, I'm not father material I'm too young Why me? Why now? Boy or a girl We should adopt The old parts are working Just when I had life sussed Think of it as a challenge This is a disaster This is amazing

This is something that happens to other people It's not fair How do nappies work? She was on the pill What if it's twins? I'm too selfish The end of my life Not the end of my life What will Mum say? It's bad luck It's good luck I can't do it I can't cope I can cope I can't . . .

He's at the pub now, watching Chelsea play Aston Villa – he supports Chelsea because the guy next to him is supporting Chelsea – and then he's at another pub spilling his guts to the Liverpool supporter and Liverpool says, 'Fuck, mate, what a fuckin disaster, fuckin hell, fuckin hell, fuck', which is a positive spin on things, but one of his Kiwi mates gets clucky, says, 'You'll be an awesome father', and another friend says to him, 'The pill doesn't work as well if you've had a curry', and everyone agrees that adoption leaves emotional scarring, so which is it to be? Emotional scarring or twenty years of child-rearing in a suburb with a mall wearing practical clothes and paying school fees and never going to the pub and ironing and nappies and dishes and housework and snap out of it, snap out of it, snap out . . .

Lots of people he barely knows confide in him about abortions, he can't believe the number, it's incredible, he realises that he is a member of the selfish generation, a generation that's been granted more freedom than it can handle, and no one has a fuckin clue what to do when all the rules are gone, and then he walks past a woman with a pram and he walks past another woman with a pram and another fuckin pram so he goes to a movie, and it's about a guy who dies of cancer but never mind, escapism is escapism, but when he comes out it's still light and his life is still his life and he's still having a baby, having a baby, and wow, Jesus, wow, sit down, remember to keep breathing . . .

*

Back in Amsterdam — that's where his return ticket leaves from — and the place is scarier than ever. He can only afford to stay in a hostel where all the occupants are gang-rapists, it's obvious just to look at them, so he hatches a plan of staying up until twelve and *then* getting stoned so he won't have to go to bed that night . . .

And that's a decision he now regrets because it's three o'clock and he's fucked to bits and a man is following him down the street saying 'Do you speak English?' and next it's 'You got some guilder, I need some guilder' and he says he hasn't got any but then it's 'I know you got guilder' and then this Turkish guy comes to the rescue with 'Hey, you leave this guy alone, he's my fren, you faaak offf faak offf' and he's gone.

Only the Turk is his friend now. The Turk says, 'What's yo name my fren?' and he says his name and Turk says, 'Where you from?' so he says 'New Zealand' and Turk says, 'Where you goin?' and he says 'Home' but Turk's not into hints, Turk says, 'I walk you, it's duk out here, danger, I walk you there' and it's all a bit Imminent Death Scene so he does a full 180-degree turn and walks in the opposite direction, and that's when Turk gets angry. 'Where you goin? are you no grateful? are you no grateful?' so he says thank you but Turk wants to make his point, 'I sav you, are you no grateful?' and Turk has turned around and caught up now, and both are walking briskly in the opposite direction from which they started. He says thank you again, but Turk says, 'On the streets we do not thank with mouths, we thank in other ways' and Jesus, Jesus, think, Jesus, and round we go again, another 180, and Turk's yelling, 'Goooo hoooome, Goooo hoooome, it's duk out here, goooo hoooome, it's no saf here, gooo hooome' and he walks as fast as he can, walking thinking Don't look back Just keep walking Don't run Stay calm Use your ears Act normal Keep walkin Fuckin Dutch Fuckin Turks Fuckin cunt Fuckin Turks — and he's in his hostel bed now, listening to the snoring symphony of a dozen intravenous-drug-using backpackers, and thinks, 'I gotta get outta here, I gotta get out, I gotta get . . .'

That night he doesn't get raped, stabbed or injected with an Aids needle. He sleeps well for three hours, gets up and heads out to the safeness of daytime, but someone has patted a 'Fuck With Me' sign on his back, cos here's another vulture pleading for guilder, so he goes through his bag of tricks: the Gradual Accelerate, the Look Away, the 180 Turn, the second 180 Turn, the Head For People, but he can't shake this fucker off, so he runs, like Rod Dixon or John Walker or Dick Quax or Peter Snell and oh to be in New Zealand but kiss goodbye to that cos he's going in the opposite direction from the train station, and there's no way he's turning back, not with Psycho Stalker back there, so he just keeps running, away from the station, there he goes, and twelve women with prams walk past him and it's all a bit much, a bit . . . and what the . . . ?

Funny thing, disorientation. He's been going for blocks and blocks and what should emerge in front of him but the *fuckin train station*, as if someone has dug it up and replanted it on the other side of the town especially for his benefit. And thank Christ, thank Christ for round towns, straight to the safe, on with the backpack, train to the airport and breathe easy, he may be four hours early but fuck it, it's the best four hours he's had for aaaaages . . .

The flight home lasts thirty-three hours, including a ten-hour stopover in an airport lounge in Bali. When he makes it to New Zealand, he is relieved to hear the accent again, he almost wants to shake hands with the nice Customs man rummaging through his backpack. When he arrives in Wellington, his girlfriend is waiting for him. She has shrunk – she always does when he goes away, it's a scientific thing – he forgets how short she is so that when he sees her again it creates the optical illusion that she is actually shorter. Her belly isn't as huge as he imagined either, he was expecting . . . what was he expecting? They are pleased to see each other and the hug is of high quality as one would expect in such a situation.

> *Pele yells we're outta here,*
> *Zina says right on,*
> *Makin moves and startin grooves,*
> *Before they know we're gone,*
>
> *Jumped into the Chevy,*
> *headed for the lights,*
> *wanna know the rest,*
> *hey buy the rights.*
> *How bizarre . . . (Da na na, da na na, da na . . .)*

A crisis shared is a crisis halved. Tonight he will sleep with her, they will gossip, swap stories, laugh (surprisingly) and also the other stuff – he'll hold her when she cries and she'll hold him when he cries. He will not touch her stomach – not tonight – that comes tomorrow, when he places his palm there, she puts a funnel-shaped bit of plastic on it and he hears a little, a little . . .

'Jesus . . .'
'What?'
'I can hear it!'
'Yeah?'
'. . . It's incredible.'
'What does it sound like?'
'. . . It's really fast, is that normal?'
'Yeah.'

The little critter's heart is going ba-doom ba-doom ba-doom ba-doom like a . . . well, like a little heart, a little . . . tiny heart, a little . . . fucking . . . little . . . miniature heart, and it's incredible, it's the continuation of the species, it's evolution, it's like . . . evolution, it's his flesh and blood, it's . . . his worst fears have come true, he is well and truly attached to the little fucker, like a magnet to a fridge. He wants the baby. She wants the baby.

They will have the baby.

the good thing

He does something good. This is satisfying in itself, but the satisfaction is doubled when other people tell him how good it was. It means a lot that his friends thought it was good, but it means even more when people in *the profession* thought it was *great*. Some of these people he has never met. They buy him drinks at the bar. They rave about the good thing he did. As he stumbles home drunk he runs over all the things they said to him. There are so many great bits. There was the person who said, 'I really liked the way you . . .' The person who said, 'It made me think.' The person who said, 'It spoke to me, it spoke for me', and the person who said, 'Brilliant. Brilliant. Brilliant.' He smiles as he zigzags his way down the street, and when he goes to sleep he recycles the conversations in his head. They are not quite as good as when they actually happened, and not quite as good as the second time he remembered them, but they are still vivid and exciting.

The next day he does the good thing again, but fewer people approach him to rave about it. Perhaps they are shy. It does not matter – there are still many compliments to wine and dine on: 'Well done on the . . .' 'Congrats on the . . .' 'The best . . . this year.' All these things make him smile and he stumbles home drunk and happy once more.

The next day after the good thing he waits for people to tell him how great it was, but only a few stragglers are there to marvel. They are kind. They say, 'I really liked the . . .' and, 'I loved it when you did the . . .' One person says, 'All in all it was brilliant, pity about the . . . but overall, quite superb.' He stumbles home pissed and a little perturbed. What did they mean by 'pity about the . . .'? Surely any ignoramus could tell the . . . was the best bit. Easily. He has a dream that night that this person is in the middle of the African desert and is run over by a herd of mountain goats. He does not know what the mountain goats are doing in the African desert, but that's dream logic for you.

The next day after the good thing no one hangs around to tell him how great it was. Is it because it is a Wednesday? What is so special about Wednesdays? Was his good thing as great as it was yesterday? He thinks so. He knows so. He thinks he knows so. So he goes to the bar to find someone to tell him how great he is. He finds a man who says, 'I didn't think I'd like your . . . but it's one of the best I have ever experienced.' What did he mean by 'I didn't think I'd like your . . .'? Why did he not think he would? Did someone tell him he wouldn't? Who told him? Why did they say this? Were they ill informed? Is someone out to get him? And what about 'one of the best things'? One of? One of? Where did 'one of' come from? He utters the 'one of' comment out loud, and the man says to him,

'Now now, don't be insecure' – which of course he laughs off, because if there is one thing he is not it is insecure; and besides, he does what he does because he has passion, he does not do it for critical acclaim!

Another couple of admirers tell him that they have done a lot of travelling lately and saw some particularly good things in Berlin, but 'This was the best thing in this country for the last ten years', which is partially reassuring, although he makes a mental note to himself 'Must Visit Berlin'.

The next night a woman says to him, 'It reminds me of Berlin.' 'How did it remind you of Berlin?' he asks as he pours himself another red wine. 'I don't know,' she says. 'It just *is* Berlin.' He explains he has never been to Berlin and could not possibly be influenced by Berlin, and the woman says to him, 'Perhaps Berlin has entered your subconscious', and now that he has had a few too many red wines he can't help but raise his voice a little: 'Are you implying that I am in any way influenced by anyone but myself?' 'No.' 'It sounds like you are.' 'I can't explain it. Perhaps if you went to Berlin.' 'Look. I will *never* go to Berlin. I hate what they do in Berlin. It's so infantile. I did what I did as a *reaction* to Berlin.' And the woman nods, says, 'Uh huh', looks at the clock on the wall and says, 'I have to meet someone.'

The night has gone badly. To cheer himself up he goes to the bar to find some people to tell him how great he is. Through the crowd he spies the woman who last night said, 'It made me look at it all in a new light', so he joins her table. She is with her friend. She tells her friend, 'This guy is incredible, you should have seen his . . .' and her friend says, 'Oh, it's *you* that did the . . .' and he nods modestly and says, 'It was nothing', but the woman says, 'It was the greatest thing I have ever experienced', which is *just* what he needed, and she heads to the bar to buy him a drink (he chooses red wine). He is alone with her friend now. Her friend does not ask him, 'What are your influences?' or 'How did you . . . ?' or even 'So how long did you work on the . . . ?' She talks about fishing. *Fishing*. He knows very little about *fishing*. Five other people join the table and they talk about *fishing* too. He attempts to add his two cents; he says fishing reminds him 'of being a small child at Lake Wakatipu and looking at all of the trout in the harbour', but no one builds on this anecdote; it is usurped by the guy who once caught an octopus, and the whole conversation has got away from him now. He tries to steer a sub-conversation his way by asking his original friend at the table, '*How* did it made you look at it all in a new light?' but this friend is so engrossed in the octopus anecdote that she does not even hear him. So he skulks off, pretending he has to go to the toilet, but instead he leaves the bar and zigzags home, utterly dejected.

The next morning he has resolved that it does not matter to him what people think of his . . . He is resolved to live the life of a normal human being again, so he goes out and buys a newspaper, and there is a newspaper review of his great thing which says that it was 'Brilliant in parts, but at times lacked maturity.'

Of course this throws him into a huge depression, and that night he does his greatest thing so far to prove them wrong, but afterwards at the bar all his 'friends' start talking about *summer* and *barbecues* and he thinks to himself, 'Has this had no effect on you, you morons?' and eight red wines later he is crying into one of his friends' shoulders, saying, 'Do you care about me for who I am or for what I do?' His friend says, 'The two things are inseparable. You are who you are because of what you do', and he storms out of the bar, screaming, 'You're all so fickle!' in a high-pitched squeal.

Next he is sprinting away from his friend who is running after him. And now the whole table is running after him saying, 'Are you all right?' and 'We love you' and 'Sorry', and one person says, 'Promise me you won't do anything stupid', and it's embarrassing, it's too embarrassing, it's all far too embarrassing . . .

The next day he cannot face any of them. When they try to talk to him he looks up at the sky as if he is in deep thought, so they say to each other, 'I think he wants to be alone', and may God strike them down for not persevering with him – if they'd cared they would have persevered – and that afternoon he phones each and every one of them because he knows they are out; he puts on a deep, pompous voice and into each answerphone he utters a single phrase: 'Shallow . . . Shallow . . . Shallow'.

He goes through his concertina files hunting for the phone numbers of his old school friends – at least they appreciated him for *who he was* – but after a fruitless search he realises he had no school friends. So he doodles on a piece of paper, *The school system is fucked*. He punctuates it with an exclamation mark, and pins it to his wall directly above the alarm clock. Then he mutters out loud, 'I do what I do for the community, but the community does *nothing* for me.' Then he harrumphs ironically, realises no one else is in the room to hear the irony of his harrumph, he thinks of having sex with nuns and drifts off to a relaxing afternoon sleep.

That night he does The Good Thing one last time, and one last time it truly is great. He knows this is not his clouded judgement because he is his own best critic. He fears seeing his friends, but they are all very supportive – they give him hugs and he apologises for being rude last night and for the answerphone messages, and his friends are kind and understanding but do offer the advice, 'You really should get out of town for a while.' He replies cryptically, 'When the time is right, the bird takes flight.'

Then he downs a whisky and spills his fourth red wine over the man who is saying, 'How old are you? It is remarkably mature', and he smiles and thinks to himself, 'Take that, critic, not that your opinion has any effect on me', and four wines later he is mumbling to his friends, 'Did you really think it was great or were you just saying that?' and his friends say, 'It really was great.' He sheds a tear and says, 'I feel very emotional at the moment, and my back is killing me', and a strange bald woman gives him a massage as he smokes a joint and rambles on about 'the cyclic nature of all things breathing . . .'

It is all over now. He has a lot of spare time, which terrifies him. He is bored with the incestuous community of his friends, so he catches a train to the new town where he can walk around anonymously, unhindered by fame.

And he is in the new town now.
And he is walking down the main street.
No one knows his name.
He thinks, 'Perfect.'
No one knows his face.
'Perfect.'
No one knows his accomplishments.
He thinks, 'Good.
This is good.
This *really* is *so* good.
It definitely irrevocably *must be* good.'
He wishes someone would talk to him.
'But that's okay.
In fact, it's *good*.
Do you know my name?
Do you know who I am?
I did a *good thing*.
Many people said it was a *great* thing.
You haven't heard of it?
Good. That's how I prefer it.

It really was a *major* accomplishment.
I have a copy on video.
It's here in my bag.
Everybody, I have a copy in my bag!
Perhaps we could all watch it together.
Everybody, *look what I've done!*
Everybody? Somebody?
Hello?'
He sighs and bites into his raspberry muffin, opens the newspaper, attempts to do the crossword, fails to get 6 Across, and sulks into his latte.

COWS

I went to a sperm bank the other day and my genes have been spliced into a new generation of cow. There's a whole herd of them, all with a part of me, eating bits of grass like a normal group of cows. But there are some giveaways: they are often late, they are unenthused and listless, they have an unkept quality about them, and they appear to be anti-establishment, not in an aggressive 'Let's organise a rebellion' way, more in a low-key 'Maybe if we ignore the farmer he'll go away' sense.

When I pop down to the farm they always come over to me, and there seems to be an unspoken understanding between us. When I look into their eyes I am reminded of older photos of my grandmother (in particular there is a likeness around the chin). In one or two of the cows I am even reminded of old photos of me at the same age.

These cows are not aware that they carry my genes (after all they are just cows) but I am aware and I have a strange urge to *be there* for them – to help them get over their first crush, to encourage them to pursue their dreams, to advise them how to deal with problem cows.

But I know it is wrong for me to assume a mantle of fatherhood. They have mums and dads of their own, and I must respect that; I must not intervene with the path that has been chosen – even though it is fair to say I could provide better for them. However they were brought up on the farm, and it would be wrong for me to take them to the city and expect them to adjust to my life. It would be wrong and selfish.

I would like to understand their language (I would love to know how to say, 'I am one percent your biological father' in Moo) but I fear that English is ingrained too deeply in my blood. So I must accept that I am fated to live in a different world from my offspring, and from now on I will resist the urge to drop in to the farm to see how they are going. As much as it tears me up, I must stay away – for them and for me.

It is a hard road I have chosen. I think about them every day, and hope they are safe and happy. I have a photo of a cow on my desk at work. When someone asks me what it is I say, 'Oh, something from my past, and a part of me in the future.' I love that photo. I love the farm. I love the fences. I love the grass. I love those cows – their ears, their eyes, their coats, their teats. I love each and every one of my beautiful children.

life skills

This is it. One day at a time. **Cross each bridge when you come to it.** Don't think of all the other bridges as you cross this bridge. They will put you off. Think one bridge at a time.

Be realistic. Don't set your goals too high. If your life goal is to be happy, adjust this goal. Adjust it according to your disposition, but perhaps you should be happy to achieve 'moderate happiness some of the time'. This would be an improvement for you. Aim low and you will achieve your goals. Then you will feel like you are getting somewhere.

Don't walk with a slouch. Improve your posture. Let the world see that you are saying 'yes' to life. If the world thinks you are saying 'yes' to life, the world will start saying 'yes' to you. **Yes is your focus word this year.** Try saying 'yes' three times before breakfast, five times each afternoon, and at least another twelve times before you go to bed. Twenty 'yes's a day keep the psychiatrist at bay.

You were born in the wrong century. You were born in the wrong country. You were born in the wrong body. You were born with the wrong income. History will look back at you fondly. Of course this is not true. History will say, 'Who were you again? I'm not sure we were introduced.' **Learn to relax and accept what you are given.** Be grateful to be alive, because you are lucky – many sperm fail to reach the egg, many eggs don't hatch, you are alive by virtue of a million-to-one fluke, which makes you special, so thank God for that.

Get some faith. Faith in God seems to work for many people. It does not mean you have to wear white shirts and black trousers. It does not mean your spiritual home is in Israel or Utah. You can be whatever you want to be with God at your side. If you don't want God at your side, find some sort of placebo God. Eat larger sandwiches, because God is not there to provide extra nourishment. Maybe take up yoga. Stretching is good for body and soul. If you have no interest in God or stretching, you had better take up a racket sport. Belt the shit out of the little ball. Punish the ball. The ball is what is holding you back. Take it out on the ball. If you have no interest in God or stretching, and you lack basic hand-eye co-ordination skills, buy a set of power tools. They are a worthwhile investment. Use them on anything. Leave a trail of destruction wherever you go. There is nothing more satisfying than making a big ugly hole where there was none before.

Depression is depressing. Of course you know this, but it is an easy thing to forget. Depression is not romantic. It is extremely depressing. Okay, so maybe it is romantic. But overridingly it is very depressing. If you are not depressed and are thinking about it for a lifestyle change, a word of caution: you are about to enter a big black hole from which there is seemingly no return. Are you sure you want to go down the hole? There are other options in life. (You could take up hairdressing, for example – many hairdressers are extremely well-adjusted people.)

If you are already depressed, remember that the person who came up with the saying 'There's a light at the end of every tunnel' was a train driver and was not intending the statement to become a psychological axiom. This is not to say there is not light at the end of tunnels – there are many situations where there is light at the end of tunnels, some good (a friendly outside world, for example), some bad (like an oncoming train). But the unfortunate fact is that you are stuck in a tunnel and there is no foreseeable way out. Yoga or God are of use here, because they can be practised in the dark. Racket skills are less useful in this environment. All you can do is walk aimlessly in some direction where there may be light. It is of enormous comfort when in this situation to know that you will look ridiculous to the outside world. Don't fight it. Go with it. Try drinking more, and making an arse of yourself in public. Sighing is good, but drinking, crying and spewing on a stranger's shoulder is even better. Let the tunnel become your friend. Learn to enjoy your depression. **Become fascinated by the absurdity of life.** Daydream erotic thoughts whenever humanly possible. You will not be in the tunnel forever – it is impossible to get stuck in a tunnel for more than, say, fifty years – so be patient and take up reading, particularly long Russian novels.

Time heals. Unfortunately time takes time. If there was a way for time not to take time, the process would be easier. Knowing time will heal does not help greatly because you have to find a way of passing the time, and you can read only so many books and watch so many videos before the novelty wears off. Perhaps the solution lies in space travel.

At least you still have your health. This is of great comfort, but is impossible not to take for granted. If you don't want to take your health for granted, ask a doctor friend to put you in traction for three months. Although this seems a drastic step, it does provide a fantastic opportunity for wallowing in despair aloud. During this time you will receive a lot of sympathy from a lot of people. At the end of it you will no longer take your health for granted – you will love having the use of your limbs and will enjoy jogging and canoeing and other aerobic activities. Of course the gloss will wear off after a couple of weeks, but a couple of weeks of happiness is not to be scoffed at. If this action seems a little too drastic, try crime. Don't choose hidden, white-collar crime – choose something more tangible, like homicide, pick-pocketing or high treason.

It is important to surround yourself with proverbs, because proverbs were not made up as some passing fancy. They are usually based on centuries of life experience. You can rest assured that the less successful proverbs of history (for example 'If you ride the neighbour's horse you will be wealthy and prosperous') have been weeded out. All that are left are the goodies: Nothing is as bad as it seems. Don't make a mountain out of a molehill. Don't cry over spilled milk. Don't bottle it all up. Smell the flowers. Carpe Diem. Let the buyer beware. Hugs, not drugs. Treat your neighbour as you would treat yourself. Don't put off to tomorrow what you could do today. Cheer up.

And here is a new proverb: There is always one person in the world having a worse time than you, so smile, get a beer down you, put on the Neil Diamond CD and sing till your voice goes hoarse. They may not be good at showing it, but someone, somewhere, at some time has cared about you more than you realised. Chin up. Have faith. Things can only get better.

18 acts of love and compassion

Either the wallpaper goes or I do
– Oscar Wilde's last words (purported)

1

'They're not the same without walnuts,' he says, and I have to agree. 'Mate,' he says, 'the person who puts dried apricot on top of an afghan has no understanding of traditions. Values. An afghan without a walnut isn't an afghan. It's a mutant chocolate crunchy treat and it may be tasty but it's no afghan. I want an afghan. A real one.'

'You want candles?' I ask him, and he tokes on his joint and speaks

as he exhales. 'Can you fit that many candles on an afghan?'
'How old?'
'Twenty-seven.'
'It'll be a waxy afghan.'
'No candles,' he says, having another toke. He passes me the joint.
'Nah, I've had enough. How will you make a wish with no candles?'
'I'll close my eyes and count to ten.'
'And what will you wish for?'
'A lifetime supply of afghans.'

He has a laughing fit which turns into a coughing fit which turns into a laughing fit again, and I open the windows because it's getting smoky and the landlord's coming round soon. 'Comin to the pub?' he asks me.

'Nah, gotta date with my razor,' I say.

He looks at my hair and says, 'Yeah, you look a bit scrubby.'

I tell him he can 'piss right off'. He chucks on his vinyl jacket and buggers off out the door.

2

Sixty-year-old man smokin cigarettes wearin a black denim jacket talkin to a woman half his age at the pub. What a sad arse. Man, he prob'ly still likes the Rolling Stones and Led Zeppelin but he still tries to stay with the play. Let's face it – he looks fuckin stupid out there on the dance floor, gyrating to techno or the latest music craze, his decrepit hips swayin from side to side lookin like any second his body will come apart like badly put-together Meccano. He's balding but that doesn't stop him sleazin up to the first-year university student, sayin, 'What are ya studyin, love?' and mocking feigned interest cos he seriously thinks it might be leading somewhere. He thinks the same moves he pulled in 1924 or whenever the fuck he was a teenager are gonna work now, and he doesn't seem to be able to take subtle hints, not even unsubtle ones, like the girl leaving the pub – he's so slaughtered now he's had his eighteenth beer, and oh God, he's singin Pink Floyd now, and someone take him to a rest home and get him a walking stick and some walk shorts cos the denims do not go well with the black teeth and the wrinkles and the voice of a grandfather, and someone take him home and make him learn to phone talkback radio, cos this guy's a sad arse, half yellin half mumblin

> Hey, who wans to have a beer with me, who's in for a fuckin beer with a handsome young stud

and then singing,

> *Remember the days of the old school yard*

and then it's

> Hey Misssster, I'm not gay or anythin, but ywanna beer, yeah? How do I work thisss bitta plastic, I'm shryin to, where's the loo here, I need the loo, hey barman, d'you remember Cat Stevens, he's a monk now is'ne, he's a bloody, fuck you look like my ex-wife, you look juss like my ffffuckin ex-wife, cept prettier . . . whass happenin with this stool, this stool's movin on me, whass with the fuckin, hey, I'm talkin to you, I'm talkin to you, you young punk, you think you're ffffuckin cool or hip or rrrad or whadever the ffffuckin word is these days, but this is ffffuckin nuthin, I was there when The Who were huuuge, when Keith Moon, y'never hearda Keith Moon? Baaarman, this young kid's never hearda Keith Moon, can ya believe? *I'm not shryin to be a big sens-s-s-sation, juss talkin bout my g-g-g-generation.* Who wans a beer, my shout my shout, who wans a beer? My grandshild is

Discuss 'the rat race', 'perspective' and let slip that you enjoy feeding ducks.

Appear sad in all the places you used to walk the dog.

Leave a trail of destruction wherever you go.

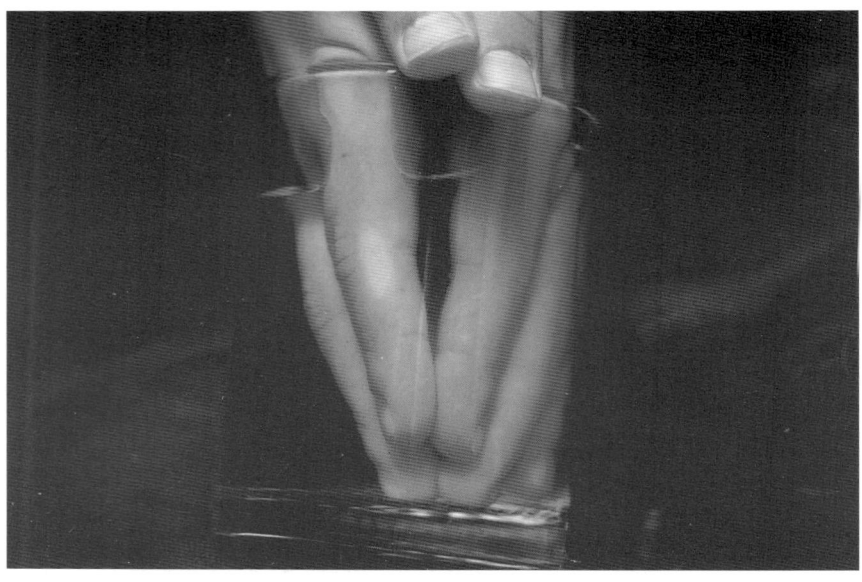

It's not your fault. You can't help the way you are.

She's screamin so high the car windows are about to crack.

He has an interesting conversation about cricket and what is wrong with the New Zealand team.

Open a tin of raspberry jam, and mix it with milk until it is glupy and disgusting.

Seeing her has 'reopened your heterosexual door'.

She's scrubbin it like it's got a disease.

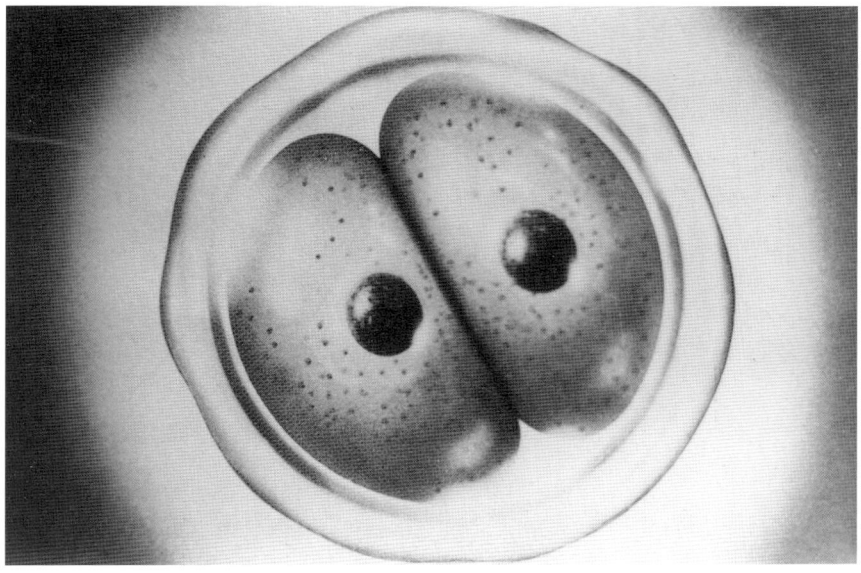

All I want is a torch.

He is going to Australia.

I say 'Increase the point size', and he says 'How big?'

Life ain't pretty at this moment in time. Life is not . . .

I'd like to make it clear that none of this is my fault.

If you go to the loo she's in your peripheral view.

I must stay away, for them and for me.

the best fffuckin grandshild in the whole — woops I farted, sorry love, but you know what they say 'bout the size of a man's fart, heh heh heh heh fffuckin dial a comedian, I'm fffuckin here free of fffuckin sharge, heh heh . . .

And here's me sittin next to him thinkin, Jesus, how do I get away, the guy's got me cornered, and whenever I try to leave he buys me another lager and I can't turn down free piss, that would be wasteful, so I'm stuck with the old bugger, he's so pissed he's practically spittin his words all over my new vinyl, rambling on about this and that and the next thing and how'd I get myself into this situation? Didn't my Mum always tell me never to accept lollies from strangers? But here I am acceptin drink after drink from this old fart who's prob'ly waitin until I'm so anaesthetised I can't move so he can have his dirty-old-man way with me in the urinal, and I'm thinkin how am I gonna get away? And I'm thinkin maybe I should say, 'I've got to get some fresh air', but he'll just follow me, he'll be like one of those dogs that followed you to school and the only way to shake it off was to stand still and pretend you were a statue; so I try that, I sit still like an inanimate object and he doesn't even notice the difference, he keeps rabbiting on about horse racing and his gambling addiction and Miss Jamaica and I'm sittin so still I can feel rigor mortis settin in, I'm sittin so still it's like I'm frozen inside a block of ice, and now I'm trapped inside the block of ice, I can no longer see the outside world for all the ice, everything's skewed and contorted like a convex mirror, and I shouldn't have taken so many drugs and that's what got me into this mess in the first place, cos I'm thinkin so fast I can't talk any more and now this old cunt's goin on to me about old speakers being better than modern ones, as if I fuckin care. I want to yell to him, 'Shut the fuck up, you decrepit old moron', but I can't because my mouth is full of beer and I was taught to say it don't spray it and maybe if I close my eyes he'll go away so I close my eyes and open them and he's still there so I close them again and open them again and it worked, it fuckin worked, because he's no longer there; instead there's a street lamp and some stars, and I can see under people's chins which is unusual because you don't usually see under chins unless you're lyin down and it looks like I might be lyin down and I am lyin down and folk are lookin down at me sayin, 'Is he all right?' 'How long's he been there?' 'We should call him a taxi', and this chick says, 'Where do you live?' so I say, '15 Schollum Road', and she says to the others, 'I live just up from him, I'll take him home', and then two guys are lifting me and woooh – careful with the hand luggage, it could explode at any moment if not treated with care – and now I'm in the back of the taxi and I'm thinkin it costs fifty bucks to soil a taxi so don't soil the taxi, don't soil the taxi, don't soil the taxi . . .

3

He's mumbling, 'Don't soil the taxi, don't soil the taxi' as we shove him in the back of the cab.

I'm scared he's gonna throw up on my dress. The driver's not helping either, he's jerking the wheel from side to side like he knows he's gonna get fifty dollars if he can make the guy vomit. I'm about to say something when the car ahead suddenly stops and the taxi driver honks his horn and turns around and says, 'If I'd hit him I could've collected the insurance; maybe next time', which makes me feel very safe thank you very much.

It's my dumb Florence Nightingale act that's got me into this mess, yet again. Will I never learn? It's like a compulsive disorder. I'm like some kind of after-hours Mother Teresa, looking after the sick and the needy – the only difference is that this lot of sick and needy have only themselves to blame. And now the guy in the back of the cab is saying, 'What's your name, what's your name?' so I tell him and he says, 'You rescued me' over and over and over again. He's kinda funny lying there, picking bits of gravel off his tongue saying, 'How did that get there?' before launching into 'If ever I'm sober and I see you on the street I won't recognise you and that's not cos I'm snobbin you, it's just that I've drunk so much I won't remember you, so I'd like to take the chance while some of my faculties are still at fifty percent to thank you for your kind act of generosity', which is a big sentence for one so wasted. I'm most impressed.

We get to his address and he wants to give me a kiss but I say, 'No thanks', so he gets out of the car and says, 'Thank you very much for your kind donation', trips on the kerb and does a face-plant on the footpath. His face is bleeding and I have to help him – I can't *not* help him – so I pay the taxi driver his fare and now I'm trying to drag this guy into his house, but he's a heavy little shit. I say to him, 'You have to help me', and he says, 'What's your name?' and I'm saying, 'Try standing up', and I put my hand on his foot and pull him up, but his vertical days are numbered because straight away he comes crashing down on top of me, like an old building in an earthquake, and now I'm trapped underneath the rubble. And he's bleeding on to me. Gross. He could have Aids or herpes or anything.

So I yell, 'Get off me', and he says, 'What?' and I'm saying, 'Get off me, I can't breathe', and then the weird little shit goes, 'The rain in Spain falls mainly on the . . .' and I say, 'What?' and he says, 'It's a test, the rain in Spain falls mainly on the . . .' and I say, 'Would you please get off me?!' and he says, 'Plain. It falls on the plain. Didn't your mother tell you rhymes?' I say to him, 'Get off me, you're hurting me!' and he laughs like he's just heard the best joke in the world while I yell, 'Get off me, get off me, get off!'

4

It's not on.

I'm trying to get a good night's sleep when there's this racket outside – I rush to see what it is and there he is on top of her, and she's screaming, 'Get off me, get off me!' Men shouldn't hit women, you know? I know everyone's entitled to their opinion but it's not right. I tolerate a lot of things but not that, I mean it's not on, it's just not on. So I drag him off her and push him up against the hedge and I say, 'Pick on someone your own size, mate!' and I'm so angry I haven't had time to get into all my clothes – I've got my PJ bottoms on but no top and I've got goose-bumps all over my chest – but I'm real pumped because I've seen this type of thing before and whenever I see a man so much as raise a finger to a woman my blood just boils. So I sock him one in the guts to teach him a lesson, and I say, 'How do you like that, huh?' and he screams, 'No, stop', and I say, 'Live by the sword, die by the sword!' and I sock him again, right in the kidneys.

The girl is screaming at me, 'Stop it, leave him alone, you idiot' – no thank-yous, no gratitude, no appreciation, nothing. I try to calm the situation; I say to her, 'Look, I know you might be in love with this guy, but he's no good for you, you can't stick up for a guy who treats you like that', which are wise words if I do say so myself and I can feel I'm on a roll so I follow that up with, 'I have a telephone inside, if you want to call Rape Crisis', and get this: she goes ape at *me*, starts hitting *me*, and of course I can't defend myself because she's a woman, so I stand there and take it, and this other little fuck starts laughing, so I say, 'Find that amusing, do you?' and kick him just below the liver.

Then Nathan comes to the door and says, 'What's going on, Dad?' I say, 'Nothing, son, back to bed', and this girl pinches me, can you believe that? She pinches me, and then the little fuckin rapist pulls my hair. Now maybe you could consider me old-fashioned but boys do not pull hair, so I yell out, 'Get off me, you faggot', and he says, 'The rain in Spain falls mainly on the steam train', and I say, 'What?!' and she says, 'I've had enough of this', and scarpers, leaving me with this guy who is bleeding – get this, bleeding on my pyjama pants, which are new last week from Hallensteins, so I yell to the kid, 'Nathan! Get us a cloth! And get me a jacket!'

5

My Dad and the Bleeding Man, by Nathan Chamberlain (8 years)

It was two o'clock in the morning. I could tell it was two o'clock because of what the clock said. I was sleeping in bed when I woke up and heard a noise. It was my Dad and a screaming girl. My Dad works at the freezing works so he is very brave. He was helping a girl getting hit by a guy. My Dad says that if a boy hits a girl then he is a sissy. My Dad told the man never to hit the lady ever again, and that if he did he would make a citizens address. I helped by getting a cloth wet, which Dad used to wipe the man's face. He was bleeding all over his mouth and the blood was red like a fire engine. He looked very very ugly, like the Prime Minister. And then my Dad told me I should go inside and go back to bed, and that's what I did. That night I had lots of interesting dreams. And when I woke up I knew that you should never hit girls. Next time you feel like hitting a girl, count to ten and then if you still feel like hitting a girl, go to the dairy and have an ice cream instead. So the moral of the story is don't hit girls.

6

Don't get me wrong, it is a good story, he has an advanced imagination for his age, but I find the subject matter a bit disturbing for one so young. So I raise it with his father at the Meet the Parents meeting. I say, 'Mr Chamberlain, Nathan's a good kid, he's good at maths and terrific at softball, and he's a good little writer too', and he says, 'But . . .' and I show him the story. He reads for a bit, and then looks at me, and I say to him, 'I'm a bit concerned with the subject matter . . .' and he says, 'What concerns you?'

It is, of course, very important in my profession to tread around the issues with great sensitivity, so I choose my words carefully. 'I've noticed that many of Nathan's stories delve into . . . violent subject matter', and his father says, 'And?' and I say, 'Well, there seems to be a pattern emerging', and he says, 'Which is?' and I say, 'Well, it seems that . . . how do I put this? It seems that perhaps Nathan is exposed to a touch more violence than, say, your average kid.'

He sits and stares at me. Then he looks down at his shoe. He rubs his forehead with his index finger, looks up at me again, and then forces a smile. And then he says, 'Ms Hetherington . . .' and I say, 'Mr Chamberlain?' He says, 'Are you a parent?' and he stares at me like we're having a staring contest so I return the stare, but he is better at staring than me so I look down at Nathan's story and say, 'I am a parent to all the children in my class.' He replies, 'That's not true, Ms Hetherington', and I say, 'I care about Nathan's welfare.' He says, 'Well perhaps you should think about your own welfare.'

So I ask him what he means by that comment and he says, 'I don't tell you how to teach, don't tell me how to be a parent', and I say, 'I'm simply raising concerns . . .' and then he says out loud, '*Are you a lesbian, Ms Hetherington?*' I ask him to keep his voice down because others in the hall are turning heads, but he continues, '*I've heard you're a lesbian. Is it true?*' and I tell him, 'My personal life is none of your business', and he turns around to all the other teachers and parents who are watching now and announces, '*Ms Hetherington is a lesbian!*' and then walks off, leaving me sitting at the table with a queue of parents in front of me, and I'm in tears.

A woman sits down at my desk and I have to say, 'Excuse me', and I run to the kitchen to clean myself up but I can't find any serviettes. Then Mr Graham the principal comes in and says, 'Are you all right?' and I say, 'I'll be fine.' Then he says, 'When I hired you, I knew of your . . . condition', and I say, 'Thank you for not counting it against me.' And he says, 'I have no problem with it, but it is important to protect the school's . . . reputation', and he stands there at the door, waiting for me to say something, and what the fuck am I supposed to say? So I concentrate on taking deep breaths and when I get the courage I look him in the eye and say, 'I'm a good teacher, Mr Graham', and he says, 'I know, but . . .' and he scratches his bald spot and says, 'Why don't you come and see me in my office tomorrow, say 8 a.m.', and leaves the room.

And I have to get out of here, but the only way is through the hall where all the teachers and parents of Henderson Normal are, so I shimmy out of the window, which leads me to the Jungle Gym, and nine-year-old Joey Falaniko is there and he says, 'Why are you crying, Ms Hetherington?' and I run, I run as fast as I can across the four square court, past the slide, over the pedestrian crossing and into my car. And I drive to the beach and I park there and stare at the waves as they come crashing in, and I dream of taking off all my clothes and running out into the surf, until the waves engulf me and the salt stings my eyes but I keep them open because I don't care, because it's green and beautiful and there's seaweed and fish and sand all around me. I dream of being a mermaid and swimming all the way to Tonga or Papua New Guinea or Moruroa or anywhere, anywhere in the

Pacific, anywhere where there is sun and calm and no people poking their noses into your business. I dream of being anywhere but here.

7

I'm porkin Katrina in the front seat of the Corolla out at Scorching Bay, and I tell ya, she's hot for it. She's moanin, 'Come on, Steve, stick your dick in my mouth', so I woop it out and it's hard as rock, hard as fuckin granite, lookin primed and ready like a rocket ready for takeoff, and she's like 'Ooh your cock looks like a big juicy rolling pin' and I'm like 'I'd like to roll your dough, baby' and she's strokin it now, and I'm tellin ya, the horse is ready to bolt. And she looks dead sexy sittin there behind the driver's wheel, her bra half-on half-off so that one tit's starin me in the face like a beautiful gift from God while the other one's playin peekaboo behind her sexy skin-toned D cup and I tell ya, it's drivin me wild . . .

I plant me arse on the steerin wheel and I'm ready to give it to her where she wants it most and she's moanin, 'Fuck me like you've never fucked before', but I say, 'You have to beg for it some more, baby' cos I'm the foreplay king and I'm capable of sustainin an erection without touchin it for up to ten minutes (that's my record anyway) and she's moanin, 'Please, baby, please', and she looks sexy there in the front seat, tomato sauce on her cheeks, and the car smells of sex and fish and chips and I'm thinkin those Chinese takeaways were the best investment I've made in a long time. And I'm lookin down at my hot dog thinkin, 'You are one sexy fuckin dork, go give it to her, baby, because she wants it, she wants it, she's fuckin spewin for it' and she's like 'Take me to heaven' and I say, 'I'll take you warp speed to planet Jupiter, baby', and I stick it in her vag real slow cos that's how they like it and she's moanin, openin her mouth like she's gettin it from a dentist, and I say, 'How you like my seafood stick baby', and she's like 'Ooh ooh ooh' and she's got hold of my butt with her sexy hands which are all greased and salty, and as I penetrate all I can think of is spring rolls and sole fillets and sweet and sour won-tons and mussels and shrimp chips and I fantasise we're in a giant vat of beef and black bean sauce and I'm gonna come any second and I do come and I unleash a primal scream cos chicks love shit like that.

And Katrina's moanin like a soprano, she's screamin so high the car windows are about to crack, and cos I'm not selfish I help her to her big O by rubbin her left tit even though I don't feel like it any more, cos that's the kind of guy I am.

And she's takin her time so I look out the car window and there's this mature woman hoppin out of the car and can you believe? She's takin off her clothes, she's takin off her – she's takin off her clothes, Katrina, and walkin into the sea, and I'm gettin hard again, I might be ready for some more action, but Katrina says, 'Do ya think we should help her?' and I'm like 'Let's do it till my cock goes blue' and she's like 'Seriously, Steve, what if she's commitin suicide?' and I'm like 'I don't know her' and she's startin to get uppy with me: 'Steve, don't be so uncarin' and I'm like 'Katrina, the only thing I care about right now is you' and she's like 'Steve' and I'm like 'You've got great tits, Katrina, they're like better than Pamela Lee Anderson's, better than Madonna's, better than the fuckin Virgin Mary's, so do ya wanna go to Jupiter again or what, baby?' and then she grabs hold of my dick with both hands and gives me a Chinese burn, can you believe, a Chinese burn, and I'm screamin 'Jesus' and she's like all uppity, puttin on her clothes, coverin those beautiful tits with her sports jacket and she's runnin out of the car towards this woman in the sea, so I follow her.

Katrina yells, 'Get away from me', so I apologise, I say, 'You know me, I'm like a horny animal. When I want it I can't think straight', and she's lookin out at the ocean sayin, 'Where is she? I've lost her', and I look out and see this head bobbin in the water so I yell, 'There she is, there she fuckin is', and Katrina's runnin after her screamin, 'Are you all right?' and the naked woman looks like she's caught in a rip and I would dive in but I can only do backstroke so Katrina jumps in and swims in her direction, and I'm thinkin, 'Jesus, this could be a situation here . . .'

So I yell out, 'Katrina, shall I phone the police?' but she can't hear me so I think for meself and run to the car so I can drive to a phone and I'm in the front seat and there's sperm on the steering wheel and how did that get there?, I must be a gymnast, and then I'm thinkin, 'Where are the keys? Where are the fuckin keys?' and Katrina's got them and I'm like 'Jesus, this is stupid' and I bang my head on the dashboard repeatedly to make myself feel better and then I see Katrina emergin from the sea with the naked woman; she's all cold and shiverin like she's got hydrothermia, so Katrina gives her her jacket which makes me fall in love with her, I mean, she's good at sex *and* charity, what more could you want in a girl?, so I say to her, 'Good on ya, Katrina, you're somethin else.'

And now she's in the car and she's fumin at me, and I'm like 'Shall we go to a movie?' and she says, 'Take me home', and I say, 'Is she all right?' and she says, 'She's fine', and I like ask, 'Did you give her your phone number?' and she says, 'What?' and I say, 'So she can return you your jacket', and she yells, *'Take me home you jerk!'* which I think is a bit of a harsh call, especially considering I was askin out of Katrina's best interests . . .

8

So he says to me, 'Are we talking A3? Are we talking A4?' and I'm waiting for him to shut up, but he keeps going on and on: 'Well, what are we talking here? A2? A3? A-what?' He keeps repeating 'A2? A3?' over an' over and so I spurt it out. 'I dropped 'im.'

That stops him dead in his tracks. 'What?' he says and I say, 'I'm no longer goin out with Steve, I'm lookin for someone more mature.'

He stares at me and then says, 'You do know what A3 is, don't you?' and I go 'Yeah' and he says, 'Half of A3 is A4, half of A4 is . . .' and waits for me to answer, so I go 'A5', and he's like 'Exactly, and so on, and so on, and so on. The reverse is also true: double A3 is of course A2, double A2 is . . .'

'I said I dropped 'im.'

'. . . A1.'

'Dean, I'm havin trouble with my mouse.'

'Oh,' he says, and leans over me. He's got the sweetest-smellin BO in the office. He picks up my mouse and turns it upside down, starts fiddling with it.

'There's your problem,' he says, and tinkers with the underside of my mouse. I turn around so that my breast is right next to his arm. 'The ball's stuck in the uh, thingamee . . . If I can just . . .' He sticks his finger in it and I lean over for a closer look so that my breast is touching his arm, and he doesn't move away. He keeps working the little ball with his finger, and finally he gets it rolling. 'There she goes,' he says, and turns the mouse over right side up again. But he doesn't let go of it, he just sits there, with the back of his arm touching my breast, none of us saying anything, so I lean in even closer. I hear him gulp and he starts frantically playing with the mouse, and we both look at the screen watching the little pointer move around all the different bits of my desktop. I'm waiting for him to kiss me but he just sits there like the virgin that he is, so I say to him, 'Dean, choose me a nice font', and he clicks on the fonts and chooses Lucida Calligraphy and I say, 'Increase the point size', and he says, 'How big?'

'Eighty.'

So he makes it eighty and taps

A4

on the screen and says, 'Perhaps forty-eight', and reduces it to forty-eight. Then I put my hand on his hand on the mouse; I highlight the A4, and I push the delete button. He says to me, 'Are you sure you wanted to do that, Katrina?' I say, 'Shhhhhh.' I move the cursor to the middle of the screen, and I type:

Dean is a spunk

And he looks at the screen and looks at me again and looks at the screen again and looks at me, except he's crying, and I say, 'Why are you crying?' and he says, 'No one's ever called me that before.' So I lean in for a kiss, but he's crying so much it turns into a hug with his head in my chest and I can feel a wet patch forming in between my breasts, and he does a big sniff and says, 'I'm sorry, I love you, Katrina, I love you more than . . . I dunno, Playstation', and he cries like a little boy.

It doesn't exactly make me horny but it's one of the sweetest things anyone's ever said to me, and I hold him so tight he can hardly breathe, but he doesn't seem to mind and I don't mind either. He can keep his face there for a whole year for all I care.

9

Efficiency.

That's all I ask for from my staff. Efficiency. I don't care what people do in their own time in their own homes; they can have sex with homosexuals for all I care, as long as it doesn't affect the work they do. But with Deano . . .

I just don't know what's got into the boy. Such a bright prospect. He can make a computer do handstands and cartwheels, our Deano can; he's the brightest prospect McEwan Copier Paper Ltd has had for years. The fact that he's my son has nothing to do with my valuations — if anything I think it's prejudiced him. I mean, when Frank Endacott was coaching the Warriors and he had his son Shane in the team, it was obvious to everyone and his dog that Shane was better suited at stand-off; but where does Frank stick him? Centre. Frank was prejudiced against Shane in the same way I am against Deano — I bet there's many a day when Deano wishes his last name wasn't McEwan. But that's the hand he was dealt, so there you go.

As I am Deano's boss as well as his father, I reckon it's bloody important to keep my two roles defined. At home I tell Deano to tidy his room, and what posters to take down, and to get me a beer, and he's allowed to give me a bit of argy-bargy, as all boys do with their dads. Ours is a special relationship — even though Deano doesn't realise it. We are very close, not in a huggy *homo* sort of way, more in a quiet 'nod's as good as a wink' *Kiwi* way.

Now at work it's different, I can assure you. He's just one of the boys (or girls — I employ girls with the appropriate skills and treat them just like boys. I'll tell you what — they're a darn sight more organised, and it's nice to have some flowers and nice smells and what-have-you around the office). So when Deano, our brightest prospect — and remember, if anything I'm prejudiced *against* him —

starts goofing off, it's important that I, as his father, treat him as a normal employee. Now, if a normal employee didn't turn up for work for a couple of days, I'd give him (or her) a stern talking to. If someone took a sickie without being sick I would take it very seriously.

Now on this day the office was already seriously depleted, given Katrina (our resource manager) was off with a bout of the flu. Now Deano's the one the whole office relies on if the computer system goes bung, since he's the only one who knows how to work the bloody things. So as you can see, this sick day dealt a serious blow to McEwan Copier Paper Ltd.

But this day I chose not to think of myself, I was busy wearing my other hat – that of concerned parent – and I went home to see Deano, who was stuck in bed with a recurrence of his glandular fever. I bought him a comic book – *Captain Marvel*, which is his favourite – and I hear him moaning in pain in the bedroom, so I rush in to help, give him CPR or Vicks 44 or what-have-you. Now blow me down if he's not *in bed* with bloody Katrina.

Now, my first thoughts were with my company hat: there in front of me, my two most reliable employees – the two I look to to set an example to the other dunderheads – *cohabitating* (and I think you know what I mean) on company time, if you will. And about a minute later I'm wearing my parent hat, thinking, 'Good on ya, kid, you're an ugly bugger and Katrina's a good-looking broad, so you must have something right with ya.' To be honest the sight left me a mite confused, so I said, 'Katrina, I'm disappointed in you. Go back to work.' And she grabs her clothes and walks out of the room in the bedsheets, but she doesn't fully think it through, does she, cos she's left bloody Deano lying on the bed without any sheets on him, naked, if you will.

Now, I make no bones about this: it's an off-putting thing. I haven't seen the boy nude since he was two, and I tell ya, the kid's all grown up now, that's for sure. I say to him, 'Deano, I know this is an odd time, but I want to take the opportunity to say you're the best bloody employee I've ever had. I was gonna wait till your birthday to say this, but bloody hell, now's as good a time as any, I'd like to formally announce that I'm renaming the company McEwan & McEwan Copiers Ltd. The second McEwan is you, Dean.'

He stares at me, then gives a little smile. I say, 'And bloody put some undies on, will ya, it's giving me the heebie-jeebies.' He says, 'Thank you, Dad', and I say, '*But* you are grounded for two weeks. No leaving the house outside of company hours, okey doke?!' He nods, then says, 'What about the Working Mens Club? I can't let you drink and drive', and I say, 'You can drop me off, then straight home. I'll taxi back.' 'Dad, that's not fiscally responsible', and I say, 'Mate, it's almost the end of the tax year. To hell with it, I'll splurge', and he grins from ear to ear.

I wander through the hallway and Katrina's got her rags back on and is about to leave the house. I stop her. I say, 'Katrina?' and she says, 'Yes?' all trembling like she's expecting to get fired. I say to her, 'Thanks for that, the boy needed a boost', and she, well, she squints at me and leaves. I go straight to the accounts book and start calculating whether the company can afford to give her a raise. Yeah, why not! It's a bloody good feeling being a boss but it's an even better feeling being a parent. I look at the photo of Deano as a nipper and I say out loud to myself, 'Ya know, Ted, you done all right. You done all bloody right . . .'

10

I place my hands underneath the hand dryer but the hand dryer's not working. So I give the hand dryer an 'extra chance', I stand there with my hands underneath it, waiting for the magic fan to kick in.

After standing there for over a minute (yes, I counted, and yes, I counted the *correct* way: one thousand and one, one thousand and two) I consider the idea of giving up, but I think of Martin Luther King and the power of peaceful protest and I wait patiently for the little electric bastard to do its job and *dry my fucking hands*.

I wait another minute (one thousand and fucking one, one thousand and fucking two) and I belt the crap out of the little machine, and V is for Victory, the hand dryer spits out two seconds of hot air, then stops again. So I hit it real hard (Mike Tyson hard), and the little fucker falls off the wall and lands on my foot. My foot starts bleeding – my ingrown toenail explodes on to the floor, and I can't put any weight on my foot. Is it broken?

I head back out to the lounge bar, where Michelle is waiting for me. She is concerned by the state of my foot. I am concerned too – I was hoping to score tonight and then this. She takes me to A&E.

The doctors are very busy at A&E. There is a guy with a dart in his head. The guy with the dart in his head is attracting a lot of attention, especially from Michelle. He is much older than Michelle, almost old enough to be her father, but I can tell he likes her. Call me paranoid but I can tell these things. The man with the dart in his head is indeed quite a charming fellow (in a docile, 'friendly dog' sort of way). I have to admit the story he tells of how he got the dart in his head is quite funny: it makes me laugh, and sends Michelle into a hysterical fit. In my weeks of intensive courting I have never seen her laugh this much before.

Is she attracted to him? Surely not. He is, after all, an older man. He is not altogether attractive. He is more likely to receive brain surgery than give it. And, I reiterate to myself, he is an older man.

I moan loudly in pain, for two reasons: (1) to get Michelle's attention, and (2) because I am actually *in pain*. I am in extreme pain, unlike the man with the dart in his head. But I am ignored –

the doctor sees to it that the man with the dart in his head is seen to immediately, even though he was after me in the queue.

As the man with the dart in the head is escorted away, he asks Michelle for her phone number. Michelle gives the man her phone number.

As Michelle walks me to the doctor's room, I try to think of a subtle way to manoeuvre the conversation around to how older men have trouble getting erections, but can't think of one. So I smile and nod as she talks about 'what an interesting man' he was. We see the doctor – he makes me sit down, and prods away at my toe. I try not to wince as he does this. I fail miserably.

I tell the doctor in a manly voice that I suspect my ankle is broken, and Michelle seems suitably concerned. I think about saying to her, 'Don't worry about me, doll', but instead come out with, 'It's sore, it's really really sore.' The doctor tells me the bad news – no broken bones, just mild bruising but I ask for an x-ray to be sure. He says no x-ray is necessary, so I insist on a second opinion. The doctor reassures me in his 'I'm a professional doctor' voice that it is only a light bruise, so I use my 'I'm not going to budge' voice and *demand* an x-ray.

As we queue for the x-ray the man with the dart in his head comes out of a small room, laughing and joking with the x-ray woman. He sees us both and asks me how my foot is. I say, 'Fine, thank you', and then the dart man proceeds to tell a joke about two horses and a talking greyhound. He is a great joke teller – he spins the joke out so that Michelle is in stitches, and when he says the punchline, 'Fuck me, a talking greyhound', Michelle is laughing so hard her back is sore. I understand the punchline and don't think it's *that* funny, but I smile politely, and then I'm called in for my x-ray. Michelle says to me, 'I'll wait out here', and the man with the dart in his head looks into her eyes and smiles.

As I get my foot x-rayed I can hear the two of them laughing in the foyer. He is using phrases like 'gives me the willies' and 'what a doozie', and I am amazed that Michelle is even remotely interested. I make a pact to dazzle her with my intelligence when I get back out, so that the difference between us will be as obvious as chalk and Chesdale cheese. The x-ray itself is uneventful (except for the x-ray woman blabbing on about her 'previous' and a hundred reasons why you should never date a cardiologist). I hobble out to the foyer, where Michelle is waiting for . . . where Michelle was supposed to be waiting for me but is not. I sit down and look for something to read. There is not a single informative magazine on offer here. (Do they think all sick people are *stupid?*) I settle for the *Woman's Day*, and feel no sympathy for Claudia Schiffer's moanings about the trials and tribulations of fame and her 'ugly duckling' childhood. None at all.

Michelle comes back four minutes thirty seconds later, and says to me, 'Ted's had his dart out' (Ted? She called him Ted), and I reply as pointedly as I can muster, 'Come out okay, did it?' and she says, 'No . . . He has internal bleeding. He's given me some phone numbers, do you have any change?' I fumble in my pocket, dredge up four fifties, and stare at my broken ankle and ingrown toenail while she phones his mother, his father, his kid, his . . . wife.

I get my x-ray back and Michelle sits beside me and asks for the verdict. 'No break,' I reply and she says, 'That's good', but then another doctor comes over our way and asks Michelle, 'Are you Mr McEwan's partner?' and she says, 'No. She's on her way', and the doctor says, 'Oh . . .' The doctor walks off again and talks to the nurse at reception. The discussion is in whispers that are too muted for us to eavesdrop on, but it is obvious by their mannerisms and demeanour that . . .

'He's dead,' Michelle says to me.
'We don't know he's –'
'He's dead. I know it.'

And she's right. You can feel it in the room. So I nod. What else can I do? I mean, what am I supposed to do?

I ask Michelle, 'Is there anything I can do?'

She says, 'Will you stay with me tonight?'

'No.'

'Please.'

'Michelle, if you knew what I'd been thinking . . .'

'I don't want to be alone tonight. Please?'

And I . . . nod. I mean, what else am I supposed to do?

Before we can go, the dart man's family arrives. I stare at them, calculating who is who – the old woman is clearly the mother, and the father is trying to calm her down. The woman talking to the doctor must be the wife, and the thin teenage-looking spotty creature pacing the floor is the son. The son is looking all around the room, like he's trying to distract himself. He's reading the notices on the walls, he's looking at his watch, he's looking at the eye chart, he's looking over at . . . me.

And I look down. And next to me, I can feel Michelle looking down as well. I mean, what else are we supposed to do? We just sit there. The two of us. In the waiting room. Unable to move, unable to talk, unable to stop listening, unable to take our eyes away from . . . my foot. My bruised, bleeding, unbroken foot.

11

I know he doesn't want to be disturbed, so I approach him carefully. He's sitting with his legs hunched up, all foetal-like, and the red light on the transmitter makes it dark one second, bright red the next. It's a pretty weird place to chill out.

'Mind if I join you?' I ask him.

'It's a free country,' he says, so I join him but keep my distance. He's quivering like a leaf.

'You cold?'

'I'm not cold.'

'I brought a blanket.'

'I'm not cold.'

'Okay . . . well I'll just . . . hmm . . .'

Truth is, I don't have a great track record in these situations; but I know it's serious, he wouldn't leave an All Blacks game at half-time unless it was serious.

'What's up?' I say, and true to form he says nothing. So I change the subject.

'Good night last night?'

'What?'

'At the pub. Was it a goodie?'

He doesn't answer. He stares out in front of him. I look up at the transmitter. 'These transmitters are amazing. Communicating images all across town . . . from, from satellites and . . . and that . . .'

'Mmm.'

'I mean, what next? One day we'll all have like, we'll . . . um . . . have like wires and . . . be able to talk to . . . um . . . anyone, wherever they are.'

'We already can.'

'Yeah, but . . . one day we won't even need phones, or anything. We'll be able to . . . um . . . do it with our minds.'

'What do you know? You can't even work a microwave.'

'That's true, I can't . . . I find them a bit . . . um . . . you know, a bit . . .'

Why am I talking about microwaves? I did not come here to talk about microwaves.

'You're missing a good game.'

He just sits there.

'Neither side giving an inch. Real tough stuff. That new lock is playing well. He's got a bit of mongrel about him. What's his name?'

He doesn't tell me his name. Another change of subject perhaps? I take a lateral tack.

'It's good to um . . . have a place to go to when you're feeling . . . you know, down. I go to the um . . . to the duckpond and feed . . . I feed the ducks and I find it quite a good place to think . . . well actually it's hard to think because of all the quacking but . . . still, the duckpond is um . . . and you've chosen this place, which is . . . interesting. You like this transmitter?'

'Yes.'

'The red light is . . . well, it's *there*, isn't it . . . if you know what I mean.'

The red light punctuates me by flickering like a fluorescent bulb turning on before going back to its old routine. I got a 'Yes' out of him, which is a start. I never know what to do in situations like this. Should I even be here? I continue: 'I find a view gives you perspective, you know, a view lets you see how small . . . people are and how small you are and your problems are . . . small from up here, and . . . it's weird when you think that every single light out there . . . except for the street lights of course, every single light . . . well maybe not petrol stations or neon signs either, but the point is . . . every single light contains a person, or people, with um . . . worries and responsibilities and . . . yet from this distance, everything they're stressing about is . . . this big.'

I hold my finger and thumb up with a street light in between them.

'In fact,' I say, 'if you hold your finger in front you can blot them out altogether . . .'

He looks at me and he holds his finger out too, blocking out all the different lights. Which I take to be progress, though he is blocking out an awful number of lights. I block out some more lights too, but I have to stop because the red light's making my vision go fuzzy.

And then he starts digging a hole. A decent-sized hole, big enough to stick your shoe into. I help him with the digging, even though I have no idea what we're digging for. He reaches into his jacket pocket and pulls out a bit of cloth – at least it's something wrapped in a bit of cloth. He unravels it, revealing . . .

Two darts.

Darts? My eyes are not mistaking me: he is holding in his hand two darts.

'These are my darts,' he says to me, and I nod. 'You'll notice there's only two of them.'

'Did you lose the other one?'

'Yes,' he says, and he's crying.

He carefully places the darts in the hole, covers them with dirt and pats the earth with his hand so it's all safely down under. Then he stands and walks toward me, stops in front of me, and says, 'This is our secret, right?'

'Right.'

'You never saw me do this.'

'I never saw you, but –'

'I hate darts.'

'Yeah but . . .'

'I'll never play again.'

'Yeah . . . but –'

'Shhhhh.' He puts his arm around me. 'Did you tape the game?'

'Yeah, of course.'

'Come on, let's go home,' he says, and we trudge off down the hill together.

12

C58. That's what the ticket says. But there's someone sitting in C58. A big guy – well, I should say a huge guy because he is literally large enough to be a . . . Unless I'm mistaken, the man sitting in my seat is . . . an All Black? Of course it can't be, but his face looks remarkably similar to the new lock's, and he's so big that . . . what else could he be? He is definitely a sportsman, and the only other possibility is basketballer, but . . . he is *definitely* an All Black. The new guy. The lock. Played in the weekend. Hard and aggressive. The new *hard man* of All Black rugby. The *enforcer*. And he's sitting in my seat.

I say, 'Excuse me' and show him my ticket. He looks at it and goes 'What?' and I say, 'I think you're sitting in . . . I think I'm sitting *there*' – and I point to the seat in the middle. He stands up to let me in.

When he stands his head almost hits the ceiling. My eye level is literally next to his huge torso – standing next to him gives me vertigo. A bit shaken, I tumble into my seat. The All Black sits down next to me. 'Thanks,' I say, and think about asking him some questions about New Zealand's big game before the intelligent part of my brain reminds me that I will have thirteen hours to think of something *original* so *Don't blow it now*.

I am now in what is traditionally the horror seat. Smack bang in the middle of two men: one an All Black and one a funny-looking guy in a yellow singlet. He has big muscles, glasses and looks about thirty. In between these hulking figures I feel the shape and size of a piece of nylon – but *Thin is in* I remind myself, before remembering that this year *Brawn is reborn, thin is in the 1998 bin.*

The man in the yellow singlet looks a friendly enough chap, and he smiles to me as I organise my bag of stuff: a couple of books, a diary, a four-in-one pen, a walkman with several hurriedly made compilation tapes, and the killer – a game of Tetris, which I intend to conquer on this long journey.

I'm sure the All Black next to me should be in first class but for some reason has ended up back here with the peasants. Now I am not usually one to endorse a class society, but it cannot be in the interests of the country to have a current All Black cramped up here. His huge legs don't seem to fit anywhere; they hang down the aisle taking up its full width, stretching up to about C56. When the trolley comes past he has to tuck them into a space where they simply will not fit, and this *cannot* be in the best interests of the national team for him to be here. I should look at his ticket and send him up to first class where he belongs – but selfishness overcomes sense of national duty, and I keep him here a while longer. After all, this is surely a once-in-a-lifetime opportunity.

I sneak the odd look in when he's eyeing up the flight attendants. He looks funny without his head gear: wisps of long brown hair munched up and fuzzy like permanent hat hair. No doubt he was a good-looking boy in his younger days, but it's hard to stay good-looking at the bottom of a ruck, and I imagine he has seen a few thousand in his lifetime. His ear is big, fat and rubbery; it looks like a surgeon has grafted a foetus onto the side of his head. I keep this thought to myself.

I ask him a question. 'Did you enjoy the game in the weekend?'

'Oh . . . yeah, it was good.'

'Were you nervous?'

'Yeah, it started off a bit loose but once we got our game plan into action, got back to basics, things started to go our way.'

'But you must have been nervous, first game and all.'

'Pretty stoked to be part of the ABs, yeah . . . I'll make sure I do the basics, get some go forward, set up a platform for the backs.'

I want to remind him that this is a private conversation, not a press conference, but I figure he has to be careful what he says. Still, he doesn't seem 'up himself', which is a nice discovery. In fact, it seems he's in the mood for talking. He looks at me and says, 'Who do you play for?' to which I have to confess 'Aah . . . no one', and he looks at me a bit confused, then nods his head slowly with an 'Ohh . . .'

He starts reading a magazine with him on the cover balancing a rugby ball on his head, and I've already read the article and know for a fact that at one point it describes him as having 'not too much up top' and suddenly here I am, sitting next to *the man himself* and I'm feeling *protective*.

'How do you find being a role model?' I ask him.

He says, 'Oh, it's good, yeah, I mean, there's nuthin like puttin on the black jersey and ah . . . I mean there's so much . . . history and aah . . . yeah, history . . .'

'How do you deal with criticism from the media?' I ask him, and he says, 'You know, ah . . . rugby's rugby an' aah, I do my talkin on the field an' . . . I just . . . concentrate on doin the basics an' . . . settin a platform for the backs, yeah.'

'Uh huh . . .'

It's beginning to feel like a long flight after all.

The flight attendant swings past with our meal, and the big lock forward hands the tray to me, and I hand it to the man in the yellow singlet, who says, 'Thanks.' He is American.

Then the big lock forward hands me my tray. Wow. This beef stew has been touched by the hand of a rugby god.

After his meal the man in the yellow singlet starts popping pills – all sorts of pills from all sorts of pill bottles. It seems I have swung into full interviewer mode now. I can't contain my curiosity.

'What are the pills?'

'A mixture,' the man in the yellow singlet says, 'Antivirals, vitamins, steroids.'

The All Black pricks his ears up.

'You must have problems getting through Customs,' I say to the man in the yellow singlet, and he shows me how he has to label everything extremely carefully for travel purposes.

'What sport do you play?' the All Black asks, and the man in yellow replies, 'I don't. I have herpes', and we never hear another word from the All Black for the rest of the trip.

Except for one time. A moment of confusion, you could call it. We are handing our trays back in the unspoken, ordered ritual that we all know: the All Black hands his back first, then I hand mine to the All Black, who hands it to the flight attendant. Then the man in yellow hands his tray to me, I hand it to the All Black, who passes it on to the flight attendant while staring at the seat in front of him. And then I notice a leftover serviette, stained and soggy with gravy, that has fallen on my lap. I attempt to hand it to the flight attendant, but the All Black intercepts it, rifles through his bag and pulls out a pen.

'Who do you want it made out to?' he says.

'Um . . . well, me I guess. Gene.'

He scrawls on the soggy serviette 'To Gene' then signs his name. He hands it back to me and I stare at it – it's too soggy from spilled gravy to put in my pocket, so I hang it from the edge of my tray table to dry.

'Shoulda given me a clean one,' the All Black says, and I reply, 'No, that's okay. Thank you', and he replies, 'No probs', puts on his headphones and returns to his magazine which, despite being only thirty pages or so long, keeps him happy all the way to LA.

13

She can go take a flying fuck. Who does she think she is? My life is none of her business. She's not my real mother. She's just another fuckin slut, another notch on Dad's bedpost. I mean, who does she think she is? 'Sometimes when you're young, Louise, you don't know what's best for you,' she says, and I'm like 'Yeah, right' – I mean, does she think she's talking to a fuckin eight-year-old? I'm seventeen, I'm fuckin seventeen, I'm old enough to drive, I'm old enough to sneak into a pub, I'm old enough to legally have sex when I like with as many people as I like, an' if I wanna fuck someone it's none of her fuckin business, is it? She can take her dumb-blonde fuckin no-brain fat arse to some other home, she's not welcome here. Even if she stays a night it's only cos Dad wants a root, so I say to her, 'Just cos Dad sticks his cock in your cunt it doesn't mean you can start playin Mum, you fat slut!' an' she loses it, she says, 'I've had a gutsful of you, young girl', an' I say, 'Woman', an' she says, 'No-hoper', so I go, 'Yeah, like, at least I've got a life. At least I don't do it with bald men', an' she does her nana big time.

She says, 'You're not so old I can't give you a smack on the bottom, young woman', an' I say, 'You lay one fuckin finger on me, I'll call the cops an' have you up for indecent assault on a minor', an' she's crying now so I go, 'Boofuckinhoo, can't handle the heat then get the fuck out of my kitchen', an' she says, 'It's your father's kitchen and he says I'm welcome here', an' I go, 'The only reason you're welcome is cos Dad needs somewhere to park his cock.'

'There's nothing to be ashamed of, Louise.'

'Just stay out of my life, okay?'

'I was trying to help, I didn't know he'd react that way', and I say, 'Are you a fuckin retard missus? I mean, Jesus, you don't go round tellin people stuff they don't need to know, it's the first law: Don't narc. Don't fuckin rat on your friends. But oh no, not you. If I say, Don't tell Dad but I've got herpes, it means don't fuckin tell Dad that I've got herpes, you dozy slut. Jesus fuckin *Christ* almighty *fuck* you're a useless fuckin no-brain barren cunt-fuckin slut.'

And that goes down like a bomb – her neck starts goin blue and she's like, 'What did you say?'

'You want me to repeat it?'

'Don't you ever say that again.'

So I say, 'Barren cunt, barren cunt', an' I open up the windows and yell to the neighbours, *'Barren cunt, she's got a barren cunt'*, an' get this – she fuckin smacks me one.

She smacks me one. Fuckin dog. Fuckin mongrel. *'Fuckin mongrel dog woof woof dog's arsehole dog fuckin piss on a lamppost dog dog dog!'* I yell, but she's backed off now, to the edge of the room, trying to control herself.

She says, 'I'm sorry that I – '

'Yeah, fuck off – '

'Shut up!!! Shut up!!! Just shut the hell up, okay?!!!'

An' I do. I mean, you would too if you saw her – fuckin bright blue an' scary like she's gonna commit murder or something. Then she says real quiet, real firm like, 'The reason I have . . . as you put it, a barren . . . The reason I can't have children . . . is that I had a sexual disease . . . and I didn't do anything about it. Now would you like me to help you or not?'

She's kinda floored me with this one. Like, 'woooh' too much information. But . . . I dunno, I . . .

I can see why she did what she did, not that I think it's okay, but I look up at her and say, 'So will you take me to the doctor?' an' she nods, and we're both crying on opposite sides of the room an' it's like . . . not embarrassing because we're both . . . you know . . . crying, and I'd like to point out that she's bawling much harder than me, she's bawling her fuckin ring out and I don't usually get into this gooey shit, but I end up holding her an' I say to her, 'Stop cryin, you dozy slut', an' she laughs, an' I laugh too. I get her some bog paper an' she wipes her face, 'cept her face is so soggy there's bits of paper still stuck to it, and usually I wouldn't say anything, I'd let her go out like that in public, but this time . . . this time I tell her an' she says, 'Thanks', and I say, 'Whatever.'

I mean, what can I say? She's still a dog, I mean, I still don't like her, but . . . but I kinda do as well. I dunno . . .

She's okay I guess.

14

She's upset, goin 'Last night was a mistake', and I say, 'Louise, the only mistake we made last night was me comin ten seconds too early for a simultaneous orgasm.'

But then she's like, 'But you're so much older than me', and I pass the Toyota on the inside and say, 'Louise, you're seventeen and I'm twenty-nine, it might seem like an age gap now, but what about when you're sixty, how old will I be then?'

'Seventy-two.'

'Exactly, and what's the difference between sixty and seventy-two? Nothing.'

I change up to fourth and take the corner with extra revs and she says, 'It's twelve years', and I go, 'Age is in the mind, Louise. I may be twenty-nine but I feel like I'm seventeen.'

Then she says the most stupid thing ever: 'But how do I know you're not on the rebound?' and I say, 'Jesus, Louise, you're much more than a rebound, you're everythin Katrina's not, you're slimmer, you're better with make-up, there's just no comparison!'

'But she's my sister.'

'No one's cheatin on anyone, Louise. You're a single woman, I'm a single man.'

'Who used to go out with my sister.'

I change down to third and pull the clutch out real slow. 'So what? She has the same last name as you – big deal. You're gonna deny your feelins just because of your last name?'

'It's not as simple as that, Steve.'

And I'm like, 'Louise, I've got a hard-on with your name on it. What could be more simple than that?'

She looks at my pants, and my cock does a big 'let me out' throb on cue, and it's too much for her – she sticks her hand on it, and it springs to life like a woken dog.

I undo me zip and unleash the rottweiller from its kennel. I turn the rear-vision mirror down so I can drive and look at it at the same time, and it makes me even hornier – I swear, it's a miracle – it's a whole inch longer than it's ever been in my entire life, and I'm like thinkin, 'Extra inch, where you been all my life?'

And Louise is jerkin me off like a seasoned professional and what could be better? I'm in third gear, goin up hills and doin tight corners while she's rubbin her hand up and down my crank shaft, goin faster an faster and I'm wonderin what it'd be like to come and do a handbrake skid at the same time, so I'm yellin, 'Faster, faster, Louise', and she takes off her top one-handed, right, and I can make out her nipples through her bra and there's a gravel patch a hundred metres ahead, there's not much time, so I yell, 'Quick, show us your tits, there's gravel ahead', and she says, 'What?' and I say, 'Quick! There's gravel ahead, I'll try and do a three-sixty', so she takes off her bra one-handed while goin at me with her other hand while I've got my foot on the accelerator and my hand on the handbrake and the timing is perfect, the gravel patch is just after the school and it looks like I'm about to do the impossible – a simultaneous orgasm and handbrake skid – when this lady with a pram steps out onto the pedestrian crossing and Louise yells out, *'Stop, Steve!!!!'*

. . . and I put my foot on the brakes and veer to the left, and we just miss her, thank fuckin Christ, we just miss her . . .

Louise is out of the car quick as a flash like, runnin after her to see if she's all right. I'm in shock and I check the rear-view mirror to see if everything's all right, but it's pointed down at my cock, and it's so big and hard that it sets me thinkin 'Waste not want not and all that', so I have a little tug so I can at least complete one of my two goals, but all I can think of was that gravel I missed out on, so I shut me eyes and think of *Baywatch* when this voice says to me, 'An' just what do you think you're doin?'

It's Louise, and is she pissed off or what! So I say, 'What does it look like? Ywanna help me?' and she says, 'I've just apologised to that lady an' her baby. I think you should do the same', an' I'm like, 'No way, she walked out after I passed the diamond. She should be apologising to me', and Louise walks off, so I follow her in the car.

She says, 'Leave me alone, I'm walkin home', and I'm like, 'Louise, it'll take you hours, let me give you a ride', so she hops in and slams the door, and we take off.

I can tell she's real angry with me, cos she's got her seat belt on. And we've been drivin for blocks and blocks, none of us sayin anythin, before finally she goes berko:

'She had a baby!'

'You were givin me a handjob. How'm I s'posed to concentrate when you're givin me a handjob?'

'You coulda killed her.'

'Derrrbrain, I was ahead of the diamond. Read your Road Code, you dozy derbrain.'

Then she says, 'Stop the fuckin car, I'm walkin, but she's left it a bit late, because her house is only a block away, so I keep drivin and she goes all high pitched: *'Stop the car!!'* I drive her to her door and wait for her to get out of the car.

But she won't get out of the car, will she? She goes, 'I wanted to get out of the car back there.'

'Well I saved you the walk.'

'Take me back and drop me off there!'

Women, you know?

So I'm like, 'All right, your highness', and we reverse back about two and a half blocks, right, at about 60k cos I like reversin real fast, and she gets out of the car, says nuthin, right, not even 'Thank you for the ride', nuthin, so I say, 'See on Tuesday, yeah?' and she goes, 'I never wanna see you ever again.'

'How 'bout Wednesday? I'll take you to Cobb 'n' Co, my shout.'

And she goes, 'No thanks. By the way, yours is the smallest cock I've ever seen.' She slams the car door and gives me the finger.

What a woman. It takes guts to say somethin like that to a bloke. It takes more than guts. It takes *balls*.

I drive past her door, I wind down the window and yell, *'I don't care if you tell the whole world I've got a small cock. Havin sex with you was the best move I ever made'*, and I plant me foot on the accelerator and roar off at 90k in a 50k zone to impress her. As I round the bend into the Limited Speed Zone I get a mental picture of her, five months from now, in a wedding dress, me beside her lookin like royalty. I chuck on Bryan Adams and hit the highway at 90 in second gear, the car's screamin and so am I: *'Lou-eeeze, Lou-eeze, You're the Beeeze Kneeeeze, You're ma Maaaain Squeeeeeze, I'm Crazzzeee for you, Lou-eeeze.'*

As I pass the Subaru Justy and tailgate the Sierra, I make a mental note to myself to leave things a couple of days to cool down, before I make my next move . . .

15

It was close.
It was too close.
I am never taking you out in public again.
I am never taking you anywhere near maniacs in cars.
From now on I will keep you inside where you are safe.
I will keep you away from electricity.
I will keep you away from heights.
I will keep you away from windows.
I will keep you away from violence on TV.
I will kiss you a thousand times every day.
There are a thousand different ways you could die, Sonya. I must protect you from every one of them.
I must be alert. I must keep my wits about me at all times.
I must shield you from pollution.
I must shield you from bad language.
I must shield you from bad people.
I will not feed you sugar.
I will have you immunised against mumps, measles, whooping cough, Aids, cancer and heart disease.
I will buy a dog to protect you. I will not let the dog near you until you are bigger than the dog.
I will take a course on mouth-to-mouth resuscitation.
I will install a fire alarm in every room.
I will install a security camera in your room.
I will pay a security guard to monitor the security camera.
I will check the security guard's life history to make sure he is not a child molester.
I will keep the security guard in a separate room, so he doesn't molest you.

I will watch the security guard at all times.
When you are old enough to go to school, I will conduct interviews with your teachers and make sure they are of sufficient quality.
I will make sure all the other children are nice to you.
If any of those children are not nice, I will make sure you *never* see them again.
I will protect you from your father.
He has been a good father so far, but people change; I must keep an eye on him to make sure he doesn't change.
Even though I love and trust your father, I will make sure he reports to me everything you do when the two of you are together.
I will make him write it on a piece of paper.
I will buy him a cellphone, and when you are alone with him I will phone it regularly.
I will phone his closest friends to make sure there is no history of child abuse in his family.
I will not let him wash you.
No one will harm you as long as you are with me.
You will sleep on your back, not your front. If you sleep on your front I will turn you over so you are on your back again.
I will not sleep.
I will keep a twenty-four-hour vigil around you to make sure you are alive at all times.
I will read a book on cot death.
You will not die of cot death.
You will not die.
You will be happy.
I will make sure of it.

16

'You're drunk,' she sssays to me, an' I saay, 'Nooo, you got it all wrong', I meean, she thinks she's so superiorior, she's never liked me, I'm an embarrassment to the fffamily, well she can get fffucked – you lis'nin to me?

Okaay, so I'd had one or two pints, but iss not like I wasss legless, I was perfecly in co'trol . . . I said to Sonya, I said to – hey punk, I'm talkin t'you, I'm talkin to you . . . Oi!

I said to Sonya, 'Here's a liddle pressie from your grandad', an' she opens it an' iss a doll, but her mother's all, 'Why di'n't you get a new one?' – she's up herself, thass what she is. I said, 'Iss the bloody thought tha' counts, isn'it?' . . . it is the thought, isn'it?, iss the bloody thought, but oh noo, not with her – Hey! Look a' me when I'm talkin to you! Look a' me when I'm fuckinnn . . . d'you want another drink? Barman, another one on me.

She takes the doll an' get thiss, she washes it in the basin, like iss dirty – as if I'd give the kid somethin dirty . . . I said, 'I washed it already, an' by washin that again you're insultin me.' Then she says, 'Is it from the tip?' an' I say, 'It doesn' matter where iss from, iss the thought tha' counts, and besides, we're not all on shriple quadruple double bloody zero-zero-zero salaries, are we, are we?'

I'm shryin to be nice, and isss all thrown back in my face, like . . . I was juss shryin to be frenly and people are so up themsel's these daysss – no I'm not repeatin mysel', I'm not repeatin – hey can I get a word in? Can I get a fffuckin word in? Thank you.

I mean, peeeeople are so up themsel's these days, specially, you know what she says? She says nuthin, not a word, not a fffuckin word, she's scrubbin the doll like iss got a disease, an' I'm like 'Whass the problem here? She likes it', an' Sonya wan's to play with the doll, but shee won' let her, will she? I say, 'The kid wan's to play with her doll', an' she says, 'Well I won' let her', an' I say, 'Scuse me, but the kid wan's to play with her doll', an' she takes the fffuckin doll an' puts it in the fffuckin rubbish bin, an' I say, *'Scuse me, the kid wan's to play with her doll!'* an' Sonya's bloody cryin and her mum's goin, 'You made her cry', an' I say, *'You made her cry, she wan's to play with her doll!'* an' Gene takes me outside, I say to him, 'That ffuckin wife of yours', an' he says, 'Calm down', an' I say, 'So you're sidin with her, are ya?' an' he says, 'P'raps you should go', an' I'm like, 'I see, I see how it is. Forgotten where ya come from, boy, huh? Forgot where ya fffuckin come from?' An' she runs out, throws the doll on the ground, breakin it, and I'm goin, 'I juss wan'ed to give the kid somethin nice, thassall', an' Gene says, 'Go!' an' I say, 'Is it cos it's got no arms? Do ya wan' me to find one with arms?' and Gene says, 'Go!' an' slams the door, like I don' exiss, an' who does he ffuckin think he is? Who does he fffuckin think . . . What did you say? What the fuck are you talkin 'bout?

What wassat?

Don' you talk t'me like that. Don't you *fuckin* talk to me like that. Where's your resspecc? Huh? Where's your ffuckin resspec, *boy! Where's your fffuckin respecc?!*

17

Foul-mouthed old-aged cunt sittin next to me at the bar. Fuck he goes on and on and on, yab yab yab this and fuckin that – look at his trap movin. Starin at his mouth makes me think of porno movies. And I stare more and think, Jesus, here I am in public starin at this guy's orifice, and he's openin and closin it in public, not carin who sees it . . .

And I start comparin his mouth to a vagina, and before I know it his mouth is a vagina, it's a talkin fuckin vagina, yabberin away, and

I'm not lookin at his eyes any more, all I can stare at is his vagina-shaped mouth openin and closin, and I shouldn'ta had that cookie, I definitely shoulda stopped at that tenth fuckin afghan, cos it's laced with some powerful shit and I don't wanna stare at this guy's mouth and see a vagina, it's sendin bad signals to my lower regions. What was in that afghan? Viagra? Whatever it was it's kicked in now, and I'm havin a beer with a talkin vagina, and I look at the barman to see if he's noticed and oh my God, unless my eyes are mistakin me the barman's beard is actually his pubic hair. He's cut off all his pubic hair and attached it to his chin to make a beard, and I'm starin at the barman's pubic beard, and the vagina next to me is sayin, 'Are you listenin to me? I'm talkin to you', and I think I've seen a new colour, I have, I've seen a new colour no human has ever seen before, it's beautiful, it's a fourth primary colour so it's not made up of any of the other three, and I'm the only one that can see it, it's invisible to the people in the real world, and it's impossible to describe but you could say there's a hint of brown and maybe a bit of pinky-green there and I've invented a new colour and how do I patent it? How do I patent a colour? Who invented the patent and how did they patent that? An old sad-arse vaginaface next to me is bleatin on about dolls or somethin, but I say, 'Hold it, I can't see the colour', and he's like, 'Whad'you say? What did you say, *boy*?'

And I'm like, 'The rain in Spain falls mainly on the plain', and he's like, 'What the fuck you talkin bout?' *And why do I think that?* Why, whenever I'm smashed, does The rain in Spain come in to my head? And why whenever I'm in the library or the video store do I always need to take a shit? And Jesus Christ, there's a shit coming out of his face now, a big shit – he doesn't realise it, so I warn him, I say, 'There's shit comin out of your mouth', and he's all anti, goin, 'Don' you talk to me like that', and I'm like, 'No, I mean it, there really is a shit comin out of your mouth', because there *is* one, and I'm tryin to warn him, I'm goin, 'Your mouth is a vagina and there's shit comin out of it', and he's like, 'Where's your ffuckin resspec, *boy!*' and he's pointing at me and his finger zaps me and for a split second he freezes me into a block of ice, too quick for the naked eye to see, but I see it, for a split .0001 of a second I am a block of ice, and no one in the real world can tell, because I'm the only one that sees everything in slow motion – there's no volume any more, like someone's pressed mute on the TV and it's quiet and sad like death and vaginaface's head is turnin into a piece of shit, his head is enveloped in shit, and every time he speaks diarrhoea comes out of his mouth, but he has no idea because the shit and the diarrhoea is all the fourth primary colour, it's invisible to him, but I can see it, and I know he can taste it so I warn him, I say, 'You're talkin diarrhoea and you don't know it!'

He thinks I'm bein rude but all I'm doin is tryin to help. He pushes me and I'm fallin off my stool now, I'm drifting in slow motion toward the floor, and it takes me like fifty seconds to hit the floor, fifty seconds of flyin like a bird, like a seagull and it's wonderful, the afghans have given me the gift of slow motion and I'm flying, and then I hit the ground and my body is havin an earthquake and all I can feel is pain, which means I'm alive and it's wonderful, so I celebrate, I yell 'I'm in pain' – and people are tryin to help me, they don't realise I'm celebratin and so I say, 'It's all right, I'm celebratin' but they're escorting me out of the pub . . .

And I'm outside the pub now, and I'm lyin on the sidewalk, but now I'm walkin, yet I'm still lyin down, I'm lyin and walkin at the same time, but I'm not walkin in the 'geographical' sense, I'm walkin in my mind, I'm walkin to a new area of my brain, cos we only use one percent and I'm off to take a look at the other ninety-nine, and I look at myself and realise somewhere along the line I've lost my body – I'm nothin but a naked disembodied cell floatin through my brain, I'm a cell and I'm floatin and I'm on a canoe, and I'm about to go down some rapids into unknown territory, and it looks a bit dark there, and I try to wade to the side but it's no use, I'm goin over the rapids and I'm scared, I can't see anything, it's all completely black like a coal mine, and I've got no torch, all I want is a torch, and I resolve that in future I'll carry a torch with me at all times because *you never know when a torch is gonna come in handy*, and I'd like to get out of here now. Could someone get me out of my head? Is there anyone out there who can get me out of my head?

And I think I'm thinkin way too much too fast too yuck now, so I'm gonna stop thinking, on the count of ten I'm gonna stop thinking and I know I can 1 do it, I know that if I 2 set my mind to it I can 3 stop thinking, that if I 4 set my mind to it I can never think 5 again, which means these are my 6 last thoughts, I'm almost at my 7 last thought, this is my last chance to 8 think, what shall I think for my last 9 thought? I need a brilliant last 9½ thought, Oscar Wilde said something brilliant before he died, he said something 9¾ brilliant, what was it? I wish I could remember what it $9^7/_8$ was. What the fuck was it? *This one's gonna drive me crazy – what the fuck $9^9/_{10}$ was it? Something to do with the curtains, something to do with wallpaper, something $9^{19}/_{20}$ profound, something extremely profound and fascinating and witty and $9^{99}/_{100}$ irreverent and provocative and profound* 10.

18

They pumped his stomach but it didn't work, so he's dead. Died on his birthday. How stylish is that? I'd like to make it very clear that none of this is my fault. I'm just the cook. When someone is stabbed, you don't blame the guy who made the knife, do you? If someone hangs themselves, you don't blame the person who made the rope. What can I say? One afghan too many. His eyes were bigger than his stomach. I told him one would be enough, but he didn't listen. He always had to push it that little bit extra. He always had to prove he was harder than the next guy. Cocky bastard. Why'd he have to be such a cocky bastard?

He told me what his wish was. He wanted the world to be a better place. I said, 'Yeah right', and he said, 'I'm serious.'

'Serious, my arse. You've got your ironic voice on.'

'What ironic voice?'

'Your "I'm taking the piss" voice.'

'I'm not taking the piss. I'd like the world to be a better place and everyone to look out for each other and no one to judge each other . . .'

'. . . and for all the children in Africa to not go hungry?'

'Yeah, why not?'

'. . . and for there to be no pain and suffering . . .'

'. . . and for everyone to be happy . . .'

'. . . and for everyone to hold hands and hug . . .'

'Yeah, why not? We all need more hugs. With my wish I'd open up a hug centre and people could come in and get their ten hugs a day free of charge and everyone would be happy.'

'Yeah, right.'

'I'm serious.'

'You're never serious.'

'Well, it's my birthday and for one day in a year I'm serious. This is for the world' and he sculls down afghan number ten.

'Well tough,' I say. 'You said it out loud so it'll never come true.'

'Oh . . . So we're all fucked then?' he asks, and I reply, 'That's right, buddy. We're all fucked.'

I wrote him a death notice. It says: 'Petherick, Richard: You got your wish after all. Now you're gone, the world's a much better place. Catch you on the other side, buddy.'

It's in this morning's paper and I like it so much I've pinned it to my wall, to forever remind me what a cunt he was. RIP buddy. RIfuckinP.

safe

If you step on a crack your mother will die, so don't step, don't step, don't step – you stepped on a crack with the toe of your right foot so now you must step on the next crack with the heel of your left – which you do, that's good, and now it's all better.

If you step in a shadow you'll catch fire, walk around the lamppost carefully, here comes a car so you'll have to jump – you jump and land safely out of shadow, but here's another so you jump and land safely again, but here's a bus, a double-decker bus, so you jump as high as you can, you catch a tree and hang there, you let yourself down when the bus has gone past. Well done, no catching fire today.

Before you can flush the loo you must say, 'Twinkle twinkle little star, How I wonder what you are.' If you don't say this you will go to hell. You must not think the next verse or – you must not think the next verse or else – don't think the next 'Up above the world so high' verse you idiot, you thought the next verse and now you are going to hell unless you sing that line out loud three times backwards – here goes: 'high so world the above Up', 'high so world the above Up', 'high so world the above Up' – there, all better; don't think 'Like a diamond in the sky' – too late, finish the last verse and reverse the whole song: 'Twinkle twinkle little star, How I wonder what you are, are you what wonder I How, star little twinkle Twinkle, sky the in diamond a Like, high so world the above Up, are you what wonder I How, star little twinkle Twinkle.' There, that's better, flush the loo, the loo is flushed so you can count to seventeen – '1 2 3 4 5 6 7 8 9 10 11 12 13 14 15 16 17' – and leave the room, phew, deep breaths, double phew, oops, you blinked so you have to blink again to make it even – that's better, itchy eye, itchy eye, have to scratch your left eye, so even it up by scratching with your right hand – good but your nose is itchy, don't touch your nose, don't touch your nose, don't touch – can't think until I've touched my nose – don't touch – can't think until I've done it – then touch your nose three times with each hand: left right left right left right, all the lefts were first and all the rights were second – need to even it up so touch again: right left right left right left – brain won't stop, need fresh air, need to stop thinking, open the door, go outside and close the door but you stood on the mat with half of your foot, so stand with half your other foot – oops you overbalanced and stepped with your left foot, so one hop with the right evens it up – good, and breathe easy, breathe easy, there's Mum, tell her you're not feeling well, say 'help' to Mum, go to the bathroom with Mum, Mum wets the face-cloth, squeeze the face-cloth tight because the water makes it all better, water makes it all better, water makes the thoughts go away and breathe easy, breathe easy, breathe easy because no one's gonna hurt you now . . .

*

Have to draw a square and have to make it perfect, out with the ruler, out with the protractor – line there, dot there, ninety degrees, perfect. Line there, dot there, ninety degrees, perfect. Line, dot, ninety degrees, line, dot, ninety degrees. Check square, oh no, square fails check because of eighty nine degree line, rub it all out, need to reverse the last two minutes so rub harder, it's no good, no good, you fucked it up, you fucked up, you fuck up, fuck up, screw up paper, take paper to rubbish bin, place it at the bottom of the rubbish bin, remember to take out every single bit of rubbish carefully so that it can be put back in exactly the same order. From left to right in a straight line on the floor we have:

>Banana peel
>Piece of toast
>Drawing pin
>Rolled-up piece of paper
>Tin can lid (messy side up)
>Onion peel
>Empty box of mixed herbs
>Coca-Cola bottle top
>Screwed up Lotto ticket
>Used cotton bud #1
>Drawing pin
>Broken glass in newspaper
>Stale potato chips
>Blonde hair, and
>Used cotton bud #2

Put in Rolled-up piece of paper#2 with bad square – naughty square, naughty square, eighty-nine degrees how could I be such an idiot – put it at bottom of newspaper, then:

Used cotton bud #2
Blonde hair
Stale potato chips
Broken glass in newspaper –

Oh no! Newspaper slips! Glass falls out! Have to rearrange glass properly – which bit goes where, must get it right or you will go to prison, must get it right, which bit goes where – here's Mum, Mum asks what you are doing. 'I'm putting the rubbish away.' She goes to put it away, you scream, 'No!' She goes to put it away, you scream, 'I need to put in in order.' She says, 'Nonsense', she goes to pick it up. 'No!' you say. She tries to pick it up but you push her away, she picks it up anyway, she's got the order all wrong, the order's all wrong, you scream, 'I'm going to prison!' You scream, *'I'm going to prison! I'm going to prison!'* You grab the rubbish bin and empty it out again, sort the rubbish, have to get the order right, Mum grabs rubbish, any order, scrambled rubbish, you scream, *'Stop it!'* Mum is putting rubbish back in rubbish bin. *'Stop it!'* You hit her, Mum's going red, Mum says, 'Go to your room!', you yell, *'I HATE YOU I HATE YOU I HATE YOU!'*, you pull rubbish out, Mum cleans up glass, the order's all wrong. You will go to prison, *'STOP IT!!!'* She's cleaning it up any order, the glass isn't right, you grab a piece of glass and stick it in her leg, Mum screams, you say, 'Sorry Mum sorry Mum.' Mum grabs face-cloth, Mum wets face-cloth – put your hands in the face-cloth, breathe easy, hands in face-cloth, water makes thoughts go away, water makes it all go away, *water makes the world go round, the world go round, the world go round, water makes the world go round it makes the world go round . . .*

In hospital with Mum because she's got glass in her leg but doctor says she's okay, and she says, 'It's not your fault. You can't help the way you are', and Mum is patting your head, saying, 'You're a good boy', 'My little prince', 'Good little boy', and you feel okay because both your hands are in a glass of water, and God promises as long as your hands stay in water you'll be okay. God will look after you as long as your hands are in the water, but you can't sleep with your hands in a glass of water so Mum lets you sleep with the wet facecloth, she says, 'Sweet dreams', you close your eyes and think of nice things like fish and candy floss and seashells and smurfs and belly buttons and chocolate and The Monster At The End Of This Book and the girl who lives down the road and double-decker buses and rainbows and cotton wool and knucklebones and bouncing balls and spinning tops and helicopters and Mum and Dad and Jesus and God and Our Father which art in Heaven, Hallowed be Thy name, Thy kingdom come, Thy will be done on earth as it is in heaven, Give us this day our daily bread, Forgive us our trespasses as we forgive those who trespass against us, Lead us not into temptation but deliver us from evil, For Thine is the Kingdom, the power and the glory, Forever and ever, Amen.

Sleep tight. Don't let the bedbugs bite.

God will keep you safe tonight.

acknowledgements

If you don't know me you will find this page boring.

I would like to thank Mum, Dad, Judy Knighton, Bernadette Murphy, Roger Hall, Lisa Warrington, David O'Donnell, Hone Kouka, Jo Randerson, Bill Manhire, Costa Botes and Brother Rob – all of whom have helped and encouraged me in my writing enormously.

Special thanks to Matt Grace, Ali Everts and Bret McKenzie – they played major roles in getting the shows up and running, for which I am indebted.

Thanks to the following people who modelled in the photos: Jack O'Donnell and Ali Everts (cover), David Suisted, Sam Auger, Hannah Clarke and Jiten Patel. Thanks also to those that helped out with the photos, and those who modelled for photos not featured in the book – sorry guys, showbiz sucks sometimes . . .

This book possibly wouldn't have happened had it not been for the Louis Johnson Award and some big cheese funding. Thanks to Cecilia Johnson and Creative New Zealand.

I dip my (metaphorical) hat to some other institutions: the Otago University Theatre Studies Department, Bats Theatre, Playmarket and of course VUP – all of whom have seen a bit too much of me from time to time.

My mum always tells me I've got good friends, and she's right. Cheers friends.

Lastly love to Stan, thanks to Lyn for being great with Stan, and a special thank-you to Mel – the best ex I've ever had, and an amazing mum too.

Everyone stand. Raise glasses. A toast to you all. Clink clink clink clinkety clink.

– Duncan